THANKS FOR THE FRIENDSHIP

Thankful Series Book Three

MELISSA BALDWIN

Copyright © 2021 by Melissa Baldwin
All rights reserved. Without limiting the rights under copyright reserved above, no part of this publication may be reproduced, stored in or introduced into a retrieval system, or transmitted, in any form, or by any means (electronic, mechanical, photocopying, recording, or otherwise) without the prior written permission of both the copyright owner and the above publisher of this book.

This is a work of fiction. Names, characters, places, brands, media, and incidents are either the product of the author's imagination or are used fictitiously. The author acknowledges the trademarked status and trademark owners of various products referenced in this work of fiction, which have been used without permission. The publication/use of these trademarks is not authorized, associated with, or sponsored by the trademark owners.

Print ISBN: 9798488259836

❀ Created with Vellum

Books by Melissa Baldwin

COZY MYSTERY

Killer Couture: A Small-Town Cozy Mystery

Poison in Paradise: a tropical romantic mystery

Movie Scripts & Madness (The Madness and Murder Mysteries #1)

Room Service & Murder (The Madness and Murder Mysteries #2)

∼

ROMANTIC COMEDY & CHICK LIT

All the Christmas Vibes: A Holiday Romantic Comedy

Love in Overtime: A Sweet Small Town Hockey Romcom (Love on Thin Ice Multi-Author Series)

Can We Talk?: A Romantic Comedy (Question #1)

I Think He Knows?: A Romantic Comedy (Question #2)

A Very Complicated Christmas: A Holiday Romantic Comedy

Unlucky Christmas: A Holiday Romantic Comedy

It Could Happen: A Romantic Comedy

Friends ForNever: A Romantic Comedy

One Way Ticket (written with Kate O'Keeffe)

Thanks for the Love: A Novella (Thankful #1)
Thanks for the Memories (Thankful #2)
Thanks for the Friendship (Thankful #3)

Love and Ohana Drama (Twist of Fate #1
Fate and Blind Dates (Twist of Fate #2)
Glances and Taking Chances (Twist of Fate #3)

On the Road to Love (Love in the City #1)
All You Need is Love (Love in the City #2)
From Runway to Love (Love in the City #3)

Fall Into Magic (Seasons of Summer #1)
Winter Can Wait (Seasons of Summer #2)
To Spring With Love (Seasons of Summer #3)
Return to Summer (Seasons of Summer #4)

See You Soon Broadway (Broadway #1)
See You Later Broadway (Broadway #2)

An Event to Remember (Event to Remember #1)
Wedding Haters (Event to Remember #2)
Not Quite Sheer Happiness (Event to Remember #3)

*I dedicate this book to my sisters-in-law and brothers-in-law.
Thank you for being so good to my siblings and for those adorable
nieces and nephews of mine.*

Chapter One

Some days I absolutely love my job, and today is one of those days. It's those moments when the stars align and everything falls into place despite a rocky journey that really gives me all the feels. And truthfully, closing this real estate deal for my clients, the Hillards, was a freaking miracle. It takes a lot to stress me out, and this particular deal had me questioning the whole meaning of life. Lots of hours and even more wine—and finally it's done.

"Cheers to Lila Barlow, real estate genius and my new best friend," Diane Hillard announces, holding up her bottle of Mountain Dew. Every time I see the woman, she's drinking the Dew.

Yuck. Of all the flavors of soda on the planet earth—that's what she chooses. I think the last time I indulged in the neon green beverage was sometime in college or on a road trip with my parents. Everyone knows you can't take a road trip without the mandatory gas station stops to get all the junk food. Regardless, Diane Hillard is obsessed. I don't think I've ever seen her without a bottle—although I guess there are worse things to be addicted to, like street drugs or reality TV.

"Thank you," I reply, flashing her a broad smile. Part of her statement is true—the part about me being a real estate genius, not us being besties.

"You earned every dime of your commission," she adds. Her husband hasn't said much, but that's typical. How could he? He's rarely able to get a word in when his wife is on a roll.

I continue with my smiling and nodding. Heck yes, I earned my commission. I'm not going to mention the endless phone calls and texts at all hours from Mrs. Hillard. I considered blocking her number for half a second, but that wouldn't have been a good business decision.

"I'm glad everything worked out, and I have no doubt that you're going to enjoy every second in your forever home." My tone is very sincere. I do wish them all the happiness in their new place.

"I've waited so long for this house," Diane says, opening her soda bottle which makes a loud hissing sound. "Have I told you about our experience back in Minnesota?"

Hmm ... only about two hundred times.

I don't have a chance to answer before she repeats the same

story I've listened to multiple times over the last few months.

Diane and her husband, Dave are officially retired and left the north for year-round sunshine and beaches. They had a miserable experience dealing with the sale of their home in Minnesota, and I've been a life savior for them—at least that's what I've been told.

"I have to text Sara," Diane announces, grabbing her phone.

Sara is the daughter of her best friend, but she refers to her as her niece. Sara's been living in Miami for a few years. Diane wants us to meet and become friends because we're both fun and spunky (her words). It's obvious she's very fond of Sara. Diane says Sara is like the daughter she never had.

"Speaking of which, I texted her yesterday, and I still haven't heard back from her." She adds, looking perplexed, "That's not like her."

I press my lips together. Poor Sara. I wonder if Diane texts her as much as she does me.

While she's preoccupied with trying to reach her, I begin to gather my things, hinting that I'm ready to leave. I'm meeting my roommates for dinner, and I'm sure the Hillards want to visit their new home now that it officially belongs to them.

"There she is," Diane exclaims, not looking up from her phone. "Aww ... she says congrats and she's excited for us."

She quickly begins typing on her phone, while her husband looks completely uninterested.

"Lila, I'm planning a housewarming party in a few weeks, and you need to come so you can finally meet Sara."

Hmm … one thing about me is that I love a good party. Food, drinks, socializing—I'm there.

"Of course, I'll be happy to stop by if I'm available," I say.

"And bring your boyfriend along."

I tighten my jaw. "Okay."

That's if I still have a boyfriend in a few weeks. Things have been pretty tense between my boyfriend Jordan and me lately. And none of it is his fault. He's an amazing man, but I'm just not sure he's right for me. Who knows though? Is there such a thing as a soulmate? I used to believe there was —I guess it depends who you ask.

My roommates, Gabby and Reagan, are both in the honeymoon phases of their relationships, but I don't think I've found my happily ever after—yet.

"Lila?" Diane calls, waving her stupid Mountain Dew in my face, the carbonated bubbles floating to the top of the bottle.

"I'm sorry—I must have zoned out," I say, snapping to attention.

"I understand. It's been an exciting day for all of us."

"Indeed. And I should get going," I say. "I'm sure you're excited to get to the house."

I rise to my feet.

"It's been a pleasure working with you," Dave Hillard says politely.

"Yes, but this is only the beginning of our friendship," Diane interjects.

She throws her arms around me and pulls me in for a tight hug. "We'll see you very soon."

I flash her a warm smile and a wave before making my exit.

Another happy client. Good job, Lila.

Like I was saying—I love my job. Helping people find their forever home is pretty fantastic.

∼

"The question is—what are you planning to do with the commission?" Gabby asks, popping a piece of bread into her mouth at dinner.

This is a typical topic of conversation for us. Gabby moved to Miami almost a year ago after her engagement ended and now works at Fun in the Sun Realty with me. She's still trying to build her clientele, and has had a rough go of it. Although lately she's started to ramp things up.

"I haven't thought it through yet," I reply. "All I can say is, I worked my butt off for this sale and the amount of relief I'm feeling right now is immeasurable."

"So true. There isn't much that compares to the minute you walk out of that title office," Gabby agrees, her hazel eyes lighting up.

I glance at my phone. "I wonder where Reagan is?"

"Oh, didn't you see her text?" Gabby asks, pushing her light brown hair behind her shoulder. "She's going to be a few minutes late because she and Jeremy are finishing up a presentation."

I snort. "Yeah, I bet they were."

Speaking of the honeymoon phase, Reagan and her co-worker are finally together, and they are completely enamored with each other. You'd never suspect they've worked together for so long before recognizing they had feelings for one another. It's a very romantic, super swoony friends-become-more story. I'm happy for Reagan because she deserves it, and so does Gabby after the hell she went through in her last relationship. The only downside is that Gabby's dating our neighbor Theo Jorgenson. I still can't believe that in a city with so many eligible men, she found him. Okay, so maybe I'm being slightly unfair. It's not that Theo is a bad person. We just have a complicated past. And not in a romantic way. *Ew—never.*

Theo's family has lived next door to mine since we were teenagers, and truthfully we just never got along. We're like oil and water, or fire and ice? You name it—we don't mix. The icing on the cake was that fateful day back in high school when Theo opened his big fat mouth and told my boyfriend Cal that he saw me kissing my ex in my driveway. Of course, he didn't have all the information and assumed there was more going on between us. I tried to explain that Brent kissed me, but the damage was already done.

Granted, Cal was going to college anyway, so it gave him the perfect opportunity to end our relationship. Needless to say, I still blame Theo. Yes, it's been a long time, but there are just some people you won't mesh with in life.

"You're probably right," Gabby says, pulling me out of my daydream. "I don't know how Reagan works so closely with her boyfriend and keeps it professional."

"Practice?" I suggest. "They've managed it this long."

"I don't think I could work with Theo."

"Yeah, me neither," I say smugly.

She scowls. "Funny. And you promised you were going to try to get along with him."

"I am," I insist. "I'm going to his birthday party, aren't I?"

"Yes," she pauses. "And Theo's really happy about it."

I take a sip of my water and swallow. "Good."

The truth is that Theo and I will probably never be best friends, but he's good to Gabby and he makes her happy. That's really all that matters.

My phone buzzes from beside me on the table. I sigh as soon as I see that it's a text from Diane Hillard. I guess the closing on their new home doesn't mean the end of her text messages.

The house is perfect. Mark your calendar for next Sunday. Small get-together at our new home.

She included a picture of her standing in front of the house, holding a Mountain Dew. Naturally.

"What's up?" Gabby asks.

I show her the picture and tell her about Diane's invite.

"She told me to invite Jordan."

"Oh."

Gabby and Reagan know about my confusing feelings for Jordan. They've listened to me go back and forth about whether or not I'm going to end things. I'm sure they're sick of listening to it—although isn't that what roommates are for?

"Have you made any decisions yet?"

I sigh. "What do you think? That would be much too easy, and you know that's not me."

Gabby giggles. "True."

"I have to do something soon. Jordan deserves to know how I'm feeling."

"Well, if it makes you feel any better, I think he'd wait until the end of time for you," Gabby says knowingly.

I bite my lower lip. "Nope, that doesn't make me feel better."

"You did choose him over Enrique."

I nod. "Yeah."

Enrique was another man I dated, but as usual my heart wasn't in it, and we didn't have the same level of attraction I have with Jordan.

"Maybe I'm just meant to be single forever—go on solo adventures, get some cats …"

Gabby holds up her hands. "Oh no, don't start in with the cats again. I can't see you with any pets, at least not at this point in your life."

I twist my long black hair around my fingers. "I'm kidding, but being on my own for a while seems like the right decision. It's time to clear my head and figure things out—I'm not being fair to Jordan or to myself. And even though I care about him, that doesn't mean we should be together right now."

Ah, why do relationships have to be so complicated? Why can't we all just find our soulmate on the first try? Hmm … that's an interesting concept.

"Well, it sounds to me like you know what you want to do," Gabby says.

I nod. "Yeah, and I'm dreading it. Jordan has told me many times that he sees a future with me."

"You tried. Don't feel bad, and forcing it will just cause issues later on," Gabby suggests.

"I know."

I really did try. I wanted nothing more than to feel that connection and hope for the future with Jordan. Some relationships just aren't meant to be.

"Sorry I'm late," Reagan announces, sliding into the booth next to me. She pulls her short blonde hair back into a low ponytail. "I'm starving. We didn't have time to stop for lunch."

Gabby and I glance at each other.

"That's what happens when you work with your boyfriend," I tease.

Her cheeks turn a shade of crimson.

"Ha, ha. Believe it or not, we're working on a huge presentation for a new client."

Reagan does marketing for an upscale hotel chain here in Miami. She also happens to work side by side with her man.

"I'm sure you are," Gabby agrees.

"Anyway, what did I miss?" Reagan asks, conveniently changing the subject away from the reason she's late.

Gabby fills her in on our discussion about me ending things with Jordan. When I think about it, I can almost feel my heartstrings being pulled.

I pick up my phone and find Jordan's number.

Hey, you. Can I come over tonight? At dinner with my roommates, but I can come straight from here.

Here we go. It's time to just rip off the Band-Aid.

"Okay, I texted him," I announce, placing my phone down on the table. "Now I need a drink."

The remainder of dinner is spent going over plans for Theo's birthday party, which of course is being held at my (our) house, my eighteen-year-old self would be in shock right now. I suppose this is what growth is all about—doing hard things. And how do I get to end a successful day? By crushing a man I care about. Being an adult is hard.

Chapter Two

As I drive to Jordan's condo, I replay what I'm going to say to him. Honestly, he shouldn't be completely shocked because we've had discussions about our relationship status on a few occasions. They usually end with him promising he'll make me fall in love with him and kissing me like I've never been kissed. Yeah—that's another dilemma. Our chemistry is pretty intense. And he's so gorgeous, with his wavy brown hair, mysterious brown eyes and a smile that could make the most miserable person happy. Kind of like Luke Perry in his Dylan McKay days. And as Reagan would say, he's super dreamy.

Anyway, I can't continue on like this. I'm a woman who's focused, confident, and always willing to go after what I want. Well, most of the time. Settling for a relationship that I have doubts about isn't me. I don't want to hurt another man—but it'll be far worse if I wait much longer.

I'm lucky enough to find a parking space right in front of Jordan's building, which almost never happens. I'll take this as a sign that I'm making the right decision. After pulling into the spot, I sit in my car for a few minutes. This isn't going to be easy, but it's so long overdue. I take a slow deep breath and head inside.

The door flies open just as I'm about to knock.

"Hi, beautiful," Jordan says, his voice deep and sultry. I force a smile as I take in his appearance. Jordan is so handsome. A former Abercrombie and Fitch model, his hair is wild, and his brown eyes sparkle behind his dark-rimmed glasses. He's wearing a pair of Adidas joggers, with a plain gray T-shirt that fits perfectly in all the right places. He holds out his arms and pulls me into his body. I follow his lead, wrapping my arms around him, and let out a sigh, knowing what's to come.

"This is a good surprise," he murmurs into my hair. "I wasn't expecting to see you until this weekend."

I pull away and press my lips together.

"This couldn't wait any longer," I say, clearing my throat.

Jordan's eyes grow wide, and he lets his arms fall to his sides. I'm sure he already knows what's coming—but that doesn't make it any easier.

"Do you want something to drink?" he asks.

Hmm ... that's not a bad idea. "Sure."

He leads me to the kitchen where he takes out a bottle of red wine.

I lean against the counter but don't say anything. We're both quiet as he pours two glasses and then leads me to the leather sectional couch. I sit down next to him and place my hand on his shoulder.

There's no point in dragging this out, so I speak up, breaking the uncomfortable silence.

"Jordan, I'm so sorry."

He holds up his hands to stop me. "Lila, you don't have to explain. I knew this was coming—you've been distant for a while."

I chew on my lip as I try to organize the words in my head. "I wish I could give you what you're looking for. But lately I've been feeling like I'm coming to a crossroads. Maybe I just need to be on my own for a while to figure out what I need in my life."

He nods slowly. "I understand. And I sure as hell don't want to continue on this path if you're not feeling it."

I nod.

"Although, we are good together," he says, brushing my cheek with his finger.

Oh, I really wish he wouldn't do things like that. I remove my hand from his shoulder and take a long sip of my wine.

Is it bad that I want him to pull me into his lap in the midst of ending our relationship?

"We are good together, which is why I've struggled with this decision," I agree. "It would be easier to stay and not let anything change, but that's not fair to either of us."

He shrugs. "I guess I wasn't thinking about that. I want to live in the now and not worry about the future."

This is why we are at a crossroads. I lived in the past for a long time and finally enjoyed every second of the present. But now my gut is telling me that I'm ready to follow a different path.

I put my hands on his cheeks. "Jordan, you are amazing. And there's a woman out there who is going to fall so head over heels in love with you some day."

"And you're not her."

I shake my head. "Believe me, I wish I was."

He leans in and places a gentle kiss on my lips. For a second I consider just staying in the moment—but I've already been doing that for too long.

"I'll really miss you, Lila," he breathes, sending a shiver down my spine.

Ugh. I wish I'd met Jordan a few years ago when I was carefree and all about having fun.

"Can you stay for a little while?" he asks innocently. "You can finish your wine, and we can just talk."

I smile. "I'd like to—but you and I both know that's probably not a good idea."

"I promise to be good. We can talk about work, and the weather."

I place my glass down on the coffee table and push my hair over my shoulder. "I can't."

He nods knowingly and pushes himself off the couch. "Come on, I'll walk you out."

As I follow him to the door, a tiny spark of doubt pops into my head. *Am I making a mistake?*

Maybe we just need a break, maybe this isn't over forever.

He opens the door and casually leans on it. "So, this is really it?" he asks.

I reach up and place a kiss on his cheek. "Good-bye, Jordan."

He gives me a pained look. "Good-bye, Lila."

My mind is spinning as I walk toward my car. I don't look back because I already know he's staring at me. Wow, why did I have to pick now to reevaluate my life and figure out what I really want?

As I make my way through the palm tree-lined streets, my brain flips back and forth between doubt and relief. I can't say that I'm not sad. Any woman with a pulse would be after giving up a guy like Jordan.

I finally pull up to the gate of my neighborhood, waving to William the guard. More relief washes over me as I make my way to my house, my safe place. There's something so comforting about being in the home I grew up in. When my parents initially told me they were thinking of selling it, it nearly broke my heart. That's when I made the decision to leave my gorgeous beach-front condo and move back home. I told them I would find roommates and keep it up for a while. I know it won't be forever—but with the way everything fell into place, I know it was the right decision.

As soon as I walk inside, I hear a man's voice, and I know immediately that it's Theo. Ugh. I promised Gabby I'd continue to try—but tonight isn't the night.

I walk into the kitchen and find Theo and Gabby with their heads together looking at something on his phone.

"Hey, Lila," Theo says cheerfully.

Gabby looks up and gives me a funny look. "Hey, how did he take it? Are you okay?"

I glance at Theo. If you asked me a year ago that I'd ever discuss anything personal with Theo Jorgenson, I'd say you were high.

"It went okay," I say, hopping up on one of the bar stools. "He claimed he knew it was coming, although he tried to get me to stay."

"Of course he did," Theo says. "He's probably having a hard time letting you go."

I sigh. "Yeah, I guess. It was the right decision, and I'm sure he'll see that soon. I can't imagine that it will take very long for Jordan to be swooped up."

"So now what?" Gabby asks, running her fingers up and down Theo's back.

Hmm ... Gabby and Theo really do make a cute couple.

"Well, I'm single for the first time in a while, and I think I'm okay with that."

She nods. "That's where I was when I moved here. After everything that went down with Dustin and Amber, I was excited to start fresh and get to know myself again."

"And then you fell out of the hammock and into my heart," Theo announces.

Gag. Did he really just say that?

"Oh, that was bad," I say with a cringe.

"It was, wasn't it?" Theo agrees. "I immediately regretted it once I heard the words come out of my mouth."

"I thought it was sweet," Gabby mumbles softly.

I roll my eyes. "On that note, I'm going to bed."

I say good night to them and make my way to my room. I fall onto my bed and let out a loud sigh. And so the next phase of my life begins. Who knows what will happen, but Lila Barlow is always up for a challenge.

Chapter Three

*D*iane Hillard is relentless. She's like the neighbor kid that constantly shows up at your house even when he's not invited.

I'm in the middle of listing three different properties, and I've gotten four texts from her in the last thirty minutes. She won't stop messaging me about her party. I personally don't have a preference between potato salad or coleslaw. And why does my opinion matter anyway?

I did break the news that I'd be attending without a plus one, and now she wants to hear all about my breakup with Jordan. I groan and put my phone all the way on the other side of my desk. As if moving it is going to keep her from texting.

"Is it true?" my co-worker Javier asks, sliding his chair over to me. He's wearing so much cologne, I'm surprised there isn't a cloud around him like you'd see in a cartoon.

"Is what true?"

Maybe I'm not meant to get much work done today. The constant distractions certainly aren't helping.

"About you and that delicious Jordan breaking up? Such a shame."

"Yep. It's true," I say without looking up from my laptop.

I'm not sure how he heard, but news travels fast in our town and especially in our office.

"I can't believe you actually went through with it." He shakes his head in judgment. Obviously he thinks I've made a huge mistake.

My phone buzzes from the other end of my desk, but I refuse to pick it up. I don't need any more menu details from Diane.

"I sure did," I reply confidently. "You know I always follow through on what I say I'm going to do."

My phone continues to buzz with messages.

"Is that him texting? Maybe he's begging you to take him back?" Javier spins around in his chair like a hyper child. But in his defense, it's part of his charm.

"No. It's my client Diane Hillard again. The woman is relentless. Clearly she thinks I have all the time in the world to chat with her."

"You shouldn't ignore your clients," Suzanna calls over her shoulder.

Javier and I both roll our eyes. Suzanna is the one agent who doesn't mesh well with the rest of the staff here at Fun in the Sun Realty. She's opinionated and intense, and honestly sometimes I don't know how she makes it in this business. She's not a people person at all, and I don't understand why she picked real estate for her profession. Our business is people.

"I'm not ignoring my client. We already closed on her property," I reply. Not that it's any of her business.

"Anyway, now that you're back in the single world, we need to go out and find some action. A single Lila is lots of fun," Javier squeals.

I make a face. "Give me a few weeks."

He laughs. "Oh, right. You probably need some time to regroup before you get back out there."

"Definitely."

"But I know you'll be up and ready sooner rather than later," he says, sliding his chair back to his desk.

I reach for my phone just in case any of my current clients are trying to get in touch with me. But of course the only messages are from Diane.

I read her latest text.

Sara's looking forward to meeting you. Her boyfriend will be here too. Maybe he has a friend he could introduce you to.

I find it so interesting that as soon as you announce a change in relationship status, everyone has "a friend to introduce you to." Especially when you don't ask. The last thing I need right now is to be set up on a blind date.

Gabby isn't in the office this morning, so I'm not surprised when I get a text from her about Theo's party. For some reason she still feels the need to give me updates and run her ideas by me. I know she's trying to be sensitive to my feelings, but it also makes me feel bad because she pays rent, so therefore it's her house too. She should be able to have a party for her boyfriend without worrying about hurting my feelings.

I send her a quick response. *That all sounds good. You don't have to run every detail by me.*

I've told her this so many times, but she still does it.

I don't respond to Diane's texts. I'm sure she'll figure out what to do about the side dishes without my help. I'll still show up at her housewarming party, and maybe after that her messages will taper off.

I continue with listing my properties when my phone rings. I'm surprised to see my mother's number. I haven't talked to my parents in a few weeks. They are currently enjoying life and traveling around the country with their best friends.

"Hello."

"Am I catching you at a bad time?" she says. "How are your sales this month?"

I roll my eyes. That's usually one of her first questions.

"Hello to you too, Mom. And I've had a pretty good month so far."

My mother is very interested in my success, which I suppose is the way it's supposed to be, right? I assume most mothers care that their children are doing well, and mine has always set the bar pretty high.

When I was a little girl, she put me in tons of pageants. At first I thought they were fun, but then over time I grew to hate them. Thankfully she didn't force it once I told her how I felt.

"Ah, very good," she says, pulling me out of my daydream. "Daddy and I will be in town next week. Are you available for dinner?"

Hmm … considering my new relationship status, I definitely have more time on my hands.

"I'll make sure I am. Just let me know which day."

"I will. We're meeting with some of Daddy's clients, but of course we need to see our baby girl."

I continue working while my mother tells me about their travels. My parents have friends everywhere and probably a lifetime supply of hotel points and frequent flyer miles, so they are loving the retired and traveling life. They also own a condo for when they come home to Miami, so they don't have to stay in our guest room. Not that they couldn't, considering the house still belongs to them. And trust me, we've had worse houseguests. One of Reagan's friends from Illinois stayed with us for a week, and it was an absolute nightmare.

"We look forward to seeing you soon. We have a lot to tell you."

I stop typing on my laptop. "Is everything okay?"

"Yes, yes. All good things."

Hmm ... the last time my parents had a lot to tell me was when they broke the news that they wanted to put our house on the market.

"Oh, Crystal is calling. I'll keep you posted on dinner."

"Mom, who's more important, your friend Crystal or your only daughter?" I ask sharply.

She chuckles before getting off the phone. I guess that was her answer.

A few seconds later my phone buzzes again with another message from Diane.

I'll have both potato salad and coleslaw, so not to worry.

Oh, good—now I'll be able to sleep without stressing over side dishes.

Great.

Diane might be over the top, but in this business it's smart to maintain good relationships. And you never know who Diane could bring into my life. Hopefully more clients, and word of mouth goes a long way in the world of real estate sales.

∼

I pull up in front of the Hillards' house, and I can already see that Diane has put her own style into the home. The porch is decorated with potted plants, large lanterns, and a massive *Welcome Home* sign. Several cars are lining the street, and I pull in behind a white BMW. I reach for the bottle of wine and check my makeup in my mirror. I'm wearing a white tank top with a long flowing black maxi skirt. My hair is full of loose waves cascading down my back.

The Hillards' new home is gorgeous, which is one of the reasons it was such a difficult sale. There were several offers on it, and I had to work my magic to make it happen.

I ring the doorbell, and a few seconds later Diane pulls open the door.

"Lila, you made it."

For some reason she seems surprised to see me. Maybe she thought I wouldn't actually show up.

She's wearing a knee-length blue T-shirt dress with the tackiest sparkly blue sandals I've ever seen. They look like an even uglier version of crocs. I know some people love those shoes, but I'm just not a fan. Are they plastic? Rubber? Does anyone really know?

"You know I wouldn't miss the first party in your new home," I say, handing her the bottle of wine.

She pats me on the arm. "That's what I told Dave, but he kept telling me not to get my hopes up. We know you're a busy girl."

I smile. "Never too busy for my favorite clients."

If there's one thing my father taught me about sales, it's to always make clients feel like they are the most important.

"Come in and meet everyone. Sara is already here."

I follow her through the house as she introduces several of the guests. She stops to pick up her signature bottle of Mountain Dew and takes a long sip.

"Sara," she calls. "Come and meet Lila."

A petite, pretty blonde woman walks toward us. She's wearing the same outfit as me—a white tank top and black maxi skirt.

"Nice outfit," I say.

"You too," she exclaims.

"See, I knew you'd hit it off," Diane says knowingly. "You're even dressed as twins."

"Aunt Diane has been wanting us to meet for months," Sara says. "She speaks so highly of you, and this house is fantastic. Thanks for all your hard work to help them get it."

Hearing this makes the hours and the countless text messages worth it.

"I'm so happy it worked out," I say. "Seeing my clients so happy means the world to me."

"I already told Sara that you and your man broke up. I'm sure her handsome boyfriend has some single doctor friends," Diane sings, elbowing me in the side.

Oh, good. I'm so glad my relationship status has been a topic of conversation.

"Well, that's very nice, but I'm taking a much needed break from relationships right now," I remind her.

"Aunt Diane wants everyone to find their lobster," Sara chimes in. "She's a hopeless romantic."

"Lobster?" I ask. "You mean like in *Friends?*"

"*Friends* is the best show ever made," Diane insists.

I guess I can't argue with that.

Sara and I chat for a few minutes and learn we actually have a few mutual acquaintances in common including my boss Elizabeth.

"I guess Miami is a smaller town than I thought," she says.

"It really is."

"My boyfriend grew up in the area, so he knows a lot of people," she tells me.

"So did I."

"Where did you go to school?" Sara asks.

"Have you eaten yet?" Diane interrupts. "Come with me. And I have to give you a tour; we're mostly settled in."

She links her arms in ours and pulls us toward the screened-in lanai before I have a chance to respond.

"It's just easier to go along with Aunt Diane," Sara whispers.

"Yes, I've learned that."

"She means well, and she has the biggest heart."

"I can tell."

Diane continues making introductions. She tells everyone that I'm her hero and the reason they have the house. I let her because—well, it's kind of true.

After a few minutes I manage to escape Diane's praise to freshen up, and as soon as I come out of the bathroom the front door opens. All of a sudden my knees go weak and I feel light-headed.

I've come face to face with my past.

Chapter Four

I've thought about this day for years. What I would say. How it would feel. Would familiar sparks return? And the answer to all of these questions is—I don't know.

"Lila?"

Say something, anything.

I've momentarily lost all ability to speak, which never happens to me. Lila Barlow always has something to say.

"Uh—hi, Cal."

"Wow, this is a surprise. It's good to see you," he says, a smile spreading across his face.

Cal Sims hasn't aged at all. I've seen pictures of him on Facebook, but it's been a few years since I've seen him in person, and that was from a distance.

As soon as I look into his familiar blue eyes, I feel like I've been transported back in time. Back to those days of my youth, a time when I didn't know what the hell life was all about. Ugh. I sound like my mother.

"It's good to see you too. How do you know the Hillards?" I ask, trying to act like I'm not phased a bit by being in his presence after all this time.

And I am wondering why he's here. Diane and Dave just moved to Miami, so I'm curious about how Cal ended up at their housewarming party.

"Hey, babe," a voice calls.

No way.

Sara joins us in the foyer and kisses Cal on the cheek.

"Oh, you two have met," she says, wrapping her arms around Cal's waist.

So Cal is Sara's boyfriend … I didn't see that coming. I guess Diane was right about us hitting it off. Not only did we show up in the same outfit, we obviously have similar taste in men.

"Actually, we go way back," Cal says. "We went to high school together."

Sara's face lights up. "Oh, my goodness, how funny. What a small world."

Yes, a small world after all. Why is the song from the Disney ride playing in my mind? That can't be a good sign. Maybe this is some weird defense mechanism. A way to deal with this strange turn of events.

"Yes, I was just asking how he knew Diane and Dave," I say. "And now I know."

I guess I could've picked up on Diane's doctor comment, but the last man I expected to be Sara's boyfriend, was a man from my past. There are plenty of doctors in Miami.

"I was just talking to Theo about you," Cal says, making my stomach do a flip.

"You were?" I exclaim.

"Yeah. The big birthday. His party is at your house, right?"

Ah. Of course, that's what they were talking about. What else would it be?

"Wait. I thought the party was at Theo's girlfriends house," Sara interjects.

I force a smile and hold up my hand. "It is. Gabby's my roommate."

Sara's mouth drops open. "This is wild. I guess our paths were meant to cross one way or another."

I nod while trying to keep my gaze off Cal. "It sure seems like it."

"We're planning to attend Theo's party," Sara adds. "I'm so happy to know that you'll be there too."

Sara tells Cal that I'm the realtor who helped the Hillards get the house. Cal and I exchange a glance, making something stir inside me.

Nope—not good.

"I was wondering where you girls went," Diane says, joining us.

"Hello, handsome," she says, putting her hands on Cal's cheeks and then giving him a hug. Clearly Diane is a big fan of Cal.

"And you've met Lila," she continues. "I was telling her that you could probably introduce her to one of those eligible doctor friends of yours—since she's not seeing anyone right now."

I grit my teeth. Why does it seem like her voice got louder all of a sudden?

"Aunt Diane, she just got out of a relationship," Sara scolds. "I'm sure she wants some time before getting involved with a new man."

Ugh. Get me out of here. Why is my personal life the topic of discussion?

"We should get back to the party," I suggest. "I don't want to keep you from your guests."

"Yes. I'm starved," Cal adds.

Hmm ... did he catch on to my discomfort? Diane obviously didn't.

"Diane has outdone herself with the food," I say quickly.

"Yes, come eat," Diane insists as she pulls Cal toward the patio.

Sara and I follow them while I take a moment to collect myself. It takes a lot to knock me off my game, and this little twist of fate has completely thrown me.

"I can't believe you and Cal know each other. Now we definitely have to get together more."

Um—once again I'm struggling for the right words. That's a hard pass for me.

"Yes, that would be nice," I lie.

Nice? Is that a *nice* way of saying it would be torture?

Thankfully there's no more mention of my current relationship status, and I end up talking to Diane's neighbor who's interested in finding a house for her son and his fiancée. My career is the perfect distraction from seeing Cal again. It's the one thing I feel like I have complete control over right now.

As soon as we finish our conversation, I decide it's time to leave. I thank Diane for inviting me and say good-bye to the rest of the guests.

"We'll see you next week," Sara says excitedly.

"Yes. I'm looking forward to it."

"Bye, Lila," Cal says, giving me a little wave.

"Bye, Cal."

When I get into the car, I lean my head against the headrest. That definitely escalated quickly.

~

As soon as I get home from the Diane's house, Reagan notices that I'm distracted, so I give her the news about seeing Cal and that he's Sara's boyfriend.

"You're kidding," Reagan exclaims, sitting up. Her short blonde hair is messy from lying on the couch.

"That's quite a—uh, coincidence."

I pour myself a glass of wine and rip open a bag of Doritos—probably not the best choice in snacks, but I've earned it.

"Yeah, you could say that."

"How do you feel?" she asks.

I stuff a chip into my mouth and chew it while I contemplate her question.

"I'm not sure. As strange as it was, I'm certainly not falling apart over it. Cal Sims has been out of my life for a long time."

She nods. "Good for you. Look at the nightmare I went through with Dante."

Reagan was in love with her friend from college, and she almost missed out on another great guy because she was holding out hope that Dante and she would end up together. It's taken me years to get Cal out of my system, but I certainly didn't stop my life over him.

"What was it like to see him again after all this time?"

I press my lips together. I don't want to read into the energy I felt with Cal for that moment. He has a girlfriend and from what I've heard, they are solid. Gabby has only mentioned Cal and his girlfriend on a few occasions. It's not a subject we talk about.

"It was fine and a little strange at first," I say. "He looks good."

Reagan gives me a curious smile. "How good?"

I laugh. "Really good. He doesn't look like he's aged at all."

"No fair," she says bluntly.

"Exactly," I agree.

"He seems to be very happy with Sara," I say. "And I'm happy for him."

"That's good," she suggests.

"Definitely. And they're coming to Theo's party." I pause. "Which I expected. Theo and Cal have been friends forever."

Reagan doesn't say anything for a few seconds. "You're a good friend. I know Gabby is so grateful to you for being okay with having the party here."

I smile. "It's fine. This is her home too. And yours."

"Yes, but she knows you and Theo have had issues in the past," she says. "You could've said no."

I shake my head. "There's no reason for that. It's a party. I'm sure it'll be fun."

I fold the top of the bag down to stop myself from eating too many chips. "Anyway, enough about that. What's up with you?"

I listen as Reagan tells me about the project she and Jeremy have been working on. I'm really trying to give her my undivided attention. There's no reason not to. So I saw Cal tonight, and he's dating Sara who seems like a great person. There's nothing else to say. Our paths have crossed again, and that's life. I refuse to overthink it.

Chapter Five

*P*ilates, friends, and real estate. Is there anything else in life? That's all I have going on right now, and I'm not mad about it. Maybe this is what I've needed for a while.

Our house is all abuzz with plans for Theo's birthday party. Gabby is loving every second of the planning process and has even made a few comments about becoming a party planner. She'd probably be pretty amazing at it too. I know she's struggled with having to restart her real estate career since moving to Miami. She left a thriving business behind when she left Central Florida. Reagan is also really enjoying the planning, and I even jumped in and helped tie ribbons around party favor bags. I also stayed quiet while Gabby went on and on about Theo not wanting her to make a big deal out of his birthday.

Yeah, right.

Theo Jorgenson has always loved being the center of attention, but I don't say that out loud.

I'm just about to walk in to my six a.m. Pilates class when my phone buzzes from inside my bag.

Hey, it's Sara, Diane gave me your number. It was great meeting you. Cal and I are looking forward to the birthday party. We have to make plans to get together soon.

I stare at the text and put the phone back in my bag. I don't need to respond to her right this second. It's not like she's a client.

I try my best to focus on my class and not think about seeing Cal again on Saturday. Not to mention that he'll be back in my home—the same home I grew up in. He's been there before. We made out in my old room which is now Reagan's room.

Gah. None of this matters anymore. The past is the past. He's happy with Sara, and I'm thrilled for them. Really.

After my class I run home to shower, and I already have six emails waiting for me when it's time to start my workday. The closing on the Hillards' home has freed up a lot of my time. I didn't realize how much of my time Diane required.

"Lila, you're on fire right now," Elizabeth calls from her office. I jump up from my chair, saunter into my boss's office, and sit down.

I really thrive on getting compliments, especially when it comes to my job. I'm good at what I do, it's one of the few things that I'm confident about. My dad always teases me that I could sell ice to an ice cream shop or something like that. I guess it runs in the family. My father worked in sales for years, and my mother also did real estate when I was young.

"Thanks, E. I guess you can say I've thrown myself into my work."

She nods as she looks at my forecast.

"I can see that—not that I'm surprised." She raises her eyebrows. "The Hillards left a stellar review. It's obvious that they think you walk on water."

I snort. "Yes, Diane still texts me. Not as frequently as when I was working with her, but more than my own mother."

"Clearly, you left a lasting impression."

"I guess so."

Elizabeth puts her pen to her lips. "Is something else on your mind?"

I shrug my shoulders. "Always. But nothing I can't handle."

I've worked for Fun in the Sun Realty for a few years, and I don't like to bring my personal life into the office. At least I try not to. Once I walk through these doors, my only focus is to help my clients find their forever home or help them sell.

"Well, keep up the great work," Elizabeth says with a smile.

"That's my plan."

"Who knows, I might have you take over this place sooner rather than later."

Huh?

"What do you mean?" I ask worriedly.

She lets out a nervous laugh. "Nothing."

My brain keeps replaying what Elizabeth said as I walk back to my desk. She started this business all on her own and she lives for it. Why would she make a comment like that?

"Hey."

Gabby's voice pulls me out of my thoughts. She's sitting at her desk, which is toward the back of the office.

"Hi," I say, walking over to her.

She furrows her brow. "What's up? You look perplexed."

Gabby actually might know if anything is up with Elizabeth because they're related—well, sort of. Her sister-in-law, Nikki, is Elizabeth's sister, which totally makes them family, right?

I look around and even though Suzanna looks busy, I'm sure her ears are wide open in hopes of hearing something interesting.

I hold up my phone and send her a quick text.

Elizabeth just made a comment about me taking over for her. She's probably kidding, but it was weird. Have you heard anything?

Gabby's phone buzzes, and she looks up at me.

I revert my eyes in Suzanna's direction, and she nods her head. She starts typing on her phone.

I haven't heard anything, but I'll definitely see if I can find out any info.

In other words, she's going to ask Nikki.

"By the way, I ran into Cal," I tell her. I haven't talked to Gabby since the Hillards' party.

Gabby's eyes grow wide. "Oh. How did that go?"

I tell her about meeting Sara.

"Wait. Sara is the woman Diane wanted you to meet."

"Yes, apparently she thinks we're a lot alike and meant to be life-long friends."

Gabby looks concerned. "That's interesting."

"In her defense, we did show up to the party wearing the same outfit."

She laughs. "Really? So you and Sara have the same taste in clothes and men."

"Yeah. Amazing, isn't it?"

She purses her lips together. "They are coming to Theo's party."

"I know."

"Is that okay? I mean—I don't want it to be super awkward."

I put my hand on her shoulder. "Gabby, I told you that it was fine."

"Yes, but that was before you saw them. Or knew about the connection to the Hillards."

Gabby looks like she might have a panic attack.

"True. But if anything, seeing them has broken the ice, and Sara seems really nice."

"Yes, she is—" She stops.

"Don't do that," I scold. "You don't have to feel weird about being friends with my ex and his girlfriend."

"I know. I just want to be considerate."

"You're always considerate."

The sound of her phone startles her. "Finally. I'm sorry I've been waiting on this call."

Gabby answers her phone, and I look at mine. There's a message waiting for me from Jordan.

Just wanted to say hi. Hope all is well.

I sigh. Although I miss him, I'm more convinced than ever that it's time for me to be on my own for a while.

After work I stop at the grocery store to pick up something for dinner. My roommates and I are hopeless in the kitchen, so most of our meals consist of takeout or easy to prepare meals. I totally live for charcuterie plates because they're easy and delish. I recently read something about them being called fancy lunchables for adults. Oh well, I have no shame.

I'm walking through the produce department when I hear someone call my name. A jolt shoots through my body.

Um.

I turn around to see Cal holding a grocery basket and a bag of oranges. He's wearing blue scrubs, which are somehow making his eyes look even more blue.

It's been years since I last saw this man in person, and now I've seen time twice in a matter of days.

"Hey," I say cautiously. "Are you following me?"

As soon as the words slip out of my mouth, I want to hide in a nearby freezer. "I'm kidding," I add before he has a chance to respond.

He smirks. "Lila, you haven't changed at all."

"I was thinking the same about you," I echo. "It's so not fair that you haven't aged."

He laughs. "I wish that were true. And you're one to talk—you look exactly the same."

I shrug. "Pilates and Botox do come in handy. Oh, and the fact that I can't cook, so I'm basically living on charcuterie plates, cereal, and wine. Not all together, of course."

"You can't cook, or you don't like to cook?" he asks.

"Both."

He nods. "My kitchen skills are average at best. Thankfully I can still stop by my parents' house because my mom is always willing to feed someone."

The memory of his mother makes me smile. "How's your mom doing?"

"She's great. Golfing and Zumba are her life now. Retirement has been good to her."

I remember Cal's mom very well. She was a teacher for years, and everyone loved her.

"Please tell her I said hello."

He nods. "I'm sure she'll be thrilled to hear from you."

Hmm ... I doubt Mrs. Sims remembers me, but I don't say that out loud.

We both grow silent, and I watch as a lady starts tapping the cantaloupes nearby.

"So, is everyone ready for the big birthday?" Cal asks finally.

I shrug. "I think so. I'm mostly hands-off of the planning process."

He nods. "Yeah. I guess you and Theo aren't exactly best friends."

And this is where it gets awkward…

"Yes, Theo and I are like oil and water. Kind of like the siblings neither of us ever wanted."

He laughs. "I hear your friendship has evolved recently."

I guess that's one way of putting it. We can be in the same room and make small talk—so I guess that means we're practically best friends now.

"We've made big strides for Gabby's sake," I say. "And after everything she's been through, the last thing she needs is drama."

Of course I'm referring to Gabby's former best friend and former fiancé getting together.

"Gabby's great, and Theo is completely smitten. I could see it the first day they met."

I nod. "That's right. The day she fell out of the hammock."

Gabby and Theo met the day she moved into my house. Long story short, he startled her which caused her to fall out of the hammock. She hurt her wrist, and Theo took her to his doctor friend, who turned out to be Cal. Imagine my surprise to hear that my new roommate met my ex on day one of living in Miami.

"Oh yeah, I knew immediately that there was a spark between them. I called it that day."

We both move to the side when a woman with a cart full of kids passes by.

"I want the cookie cereal," a little girls wails.

The woman ignores her while she begins filling a plastic bag full of apples.

"It's my turn to pick the cereal," a boy snaps.

"Anyway, the party should be fun," Cal continues.

Our silence returns. We've already discussed Theo and Gabby and the birthday party. I mean, what else is there to talk about? We're practically strangers.

"You obviously know how to get to the party," I say with a slight shrug.

A slight smile spreads across his face. "Yes, I'm familiar with the area."

"I haven't been living in my parents' house all this time," I add. "I had an amazing condo on the bay."

I don't know why I feel the need to tell him this. I'm sure he doesn't care where I lived over the years.

"That's right. Theo said you moved back in and were looking for roommates."

I tell him about my parents wanting to sell the house and how I couldn't bear it.

"I know it's just a house and they won't keep it forever, but I wanted to live there one more time before it's gone," I say with a shoulder shrug.

He puts his basket down on the ground. "I get it. My folks still live in the same house. It's comforting to go home every once in a while."

His phone starts ringing, and he pulls it out of his pocket.

"It's Sara. Hang on."

Of course, it is. *She's his girlfriend.*

I make myself busy sorting through avocados.

"Hey. Guess who I just ran into at the store."

I grab a few avocados and a bag of celery while I wait for him to finish his conversation. This trip to the market has gone completely rogue.

"Okay. See you later," he says into the phone. "Sorry about that, Lila."

"No worries. I should probably get going."

He noticeably hesitates. "Oh, yes, me too. It was nice to catch up."

"For sure. And I guess I'll see you at my house soon."

We say a quick good-bye, and I continue my shopping.

Clearly, Cal Sims has reentered my life, and I'm not sure how I feel about it.

Chapter Six

Theo is at the house when I arrive home. Why does this not surprise me? All of a sudden our lives seems to completely revolve around our neighbor.

"Hey, I was just about to text you. Theo ordered dinner for us," Gabby says.

I hold up my shopping bags. "I stopped by the store, but that food looks better than what I was going to make."

I glance at the variety of sushi, rice, and edamame spread out on the island.

"It's the least I could do for all of you," Theo says with a shrug. "Gabby's told me how much you've helped with the planning."

Hmm ... I wouldn't necessarily call tying ribbons helping, but I don't say anything.

"It's nothing," I say, putting my bags down on the counter. As I unload the contents, the sight of the package of celery reminds me of seeing Cal in the store.

Ugh. Is this going to happen every time I look at vegetables from now on?

I might as well tell them before Cal does.

"I just ran into Cal at the market," I say nonchalantly.

When I look over, I catch Gabby and Theo exchanging a glance.

"You guys can relax," I add. "That stuff is in the past. We're all grown up now."

Gabby breathes a sigh of relief, and Theo's shoulders relax.

"Anyway, tell me about the sushi. I'm famished."

After dinner I head to my room to change. I actually had a nice chat with Theo, and I know it made Gabby happy to see us getting along so well. I guess time does heal everything.

As I finish washing my face, I get a text from my mother asking if I'm free tomorrow night. I guess my parents found the time to squeeze me in to their busy schedule. We plan to meet at Bella, a family favorite of ours.

I'm excited to see my parents. As an only child, we've always been close. Even when their expectations seemed unachievable at times, I knew they loved me and only wanted the best for me. And those expectations have led to a lot of success, so I'm grateful for that.

My mother said they had a lot to tell me. The last time we had one of these dinners, I asked them to hold off on selling the house for a while. They agreed, but I always knew the clock would be ticking.

I sit on the edge of my bed, while a wave of dread comes over me. I look around the massive master bedroom that used to belong to my parents. It's probably time for me to let go of this house, I certainly didn't give it a second thought while I was counting the minutes until I was out on my own. Somewhere along the line, something shifted in me. My career flourished, while my personal life has been mostly unsettled. I always wondered how it was possible to be surrounded by friends but still feel alone.

Maybe that's why I felt the need to come home again. The safety of this house has always been a constant in my life, even when my parents weren't here. Don't get me wrong. I thoroughly enjoy having a busy social life, but as time has gone on, I've started to crave a more settled life in some respect.

A knock on my door pulls me out of my thoughts.

"Come in," I call as I pull on a pair of sweatpants.

Gabby pops her head in. "Just checking on you."

I roll my eyes. "I'm totally fine."

She sits on the edge of the bed.

"I know—but—"

"Is Theo still here?"

She nods. "He's up cleaning the kitchen. He insisted."

"Hah. Well, that definitely makes him a keeper."

Her face turns bright red.

"By the way, Elizabeth posted the sales projections. You're killin' it again. Maybe you can transfer some of your good sales mojo to me?" She gives me a half smile, but I can see the concern on her face.

"Hey, don't worry," I tell her. "Business will pick up."

She shrugs. "Haven't we been saying that for months? I feel like every time I get a win, I end up taking three steps back again."

"You had to start over. It takes time."

She twists her mouth to the side. "I'm starting to wonder if it's time for me to do something else," she says. "I've been doing real estate for so long, and maybe it's time for a change."

"There's nothing wrong with trying something new," I tell her.

"It's terrifying."

"And kind of exciting."

"Yeah, that's what Theo says."

I hold my hands up. "Well, if Theo and I are on the same page, then you know there's something to it."

She laughs. "I guess so."

"Do you have any idea what you want to do?"

She grits her teeth. "I'm not sure. I've never really thought about doing anything else."

I give her a thoughtful look. "You'll figure it out. If there's anything I know about you, it's that you always land on your feet."

She lets out a frustrated sigh. "Yeah, it seems like I've had to do that a lot in the last few years."

I really admire Gabby. She's strong and determined. I don't know how I would've reacted if I went through what she did, but she's a much kinder person than I am.

"Anyway, I just wanted to make sure you were okay."

I laugh. "You don't have to worry. I'm getting used to seeing Cal, and it's fine."

She jumps up from my bed. "Good."

"Now go take care of your boyfriend," I demand.

After Gabby leaves I think about what she said. I'm not in the same situation as she is when it comes to her career, but I like the idea of trying new things. Maybe that's how I need to look at life in general. I'm definitely at a crossroads, and it's time to reevaluate.

But first I need to have dinner with my parents. It will be nice to see them.

～

When I was a little girl, I distinctly remember the period of time my mother sold homes. One of my favorite things to do was go to open houses and tour model homes. There was just something so exhilarating about it, and I think that's when my love for real estate was born. I considered other careers, but I do much better if I'm able to manage myself. And even though Elizabeth is my boss, she's mostly hands-off when it comes to managing me.

I pop in and out of the office a few times in between meeting with clients, and before I know it, I'm sitting in Bella waiting for my parents. I'm wearing a cap sleeve white T-shirt with high-waisted, pinstriped pants. It may seem silly to care about my outfit because it's dinner with my family. But it's important, especially to my mother.

I'm about to request a table, when the door flies open. I immediately take in my mother's familiar scent. The same perfume she's worn for as long as I can remember.

She's wearing a knee-length navy blue dress, with a pair of gorgeous wedges that look perfect on her tanned and toned legs.

My mother is stunning—yes, she's had some help in keeping the wrinkles under control, but she still looks fantastic.

"There she is," my dad says excitedly. My father looks great too. Tall, lean, and his wrinkles look minimal as well, not that I'm surprised. My mom takes good care of him.

I hurry to my parents and throw my arms around both of them. In this moment it hits me just how much I miss them.

"You look wonderful," my mother says. "And your hair looks very healthy."

She runs her fingers through the strands and examines the ends closely. Like I would actually show up to see my mother with split ends.

"Thanks, Mom."

The host leads us to a table, and we sit down. I immediately ask them about their recent travels. I know how much they love talking about them, and I'm genuinely interested. Someday I'd love to do the same, whether it be with my husband or solo. Apparently solo trips are super popular right now. I met a woman from Germany at a party recently who has done two separate solo trips here in the states. She told me about how much she loved having the freedom to go wherever she wanted at any time.

"You should join us sometime," my dad says, pulling me out of my thoughts. "We're heading to New York soon."

I smile. "I do love Manhattan."

"Oh, you should," my mother exclaims. "When's the last time you took some time off work?"

Hmm ... I'd have to think about this. The last trip I had was a quick weekend getaway with friends in Islamorada on my friend Paul's boat. It was fun, but it wasn't an actual vacation. I'm probably long overdue, and maybe a trip with my parents would be good for me right now.

"I definitely have some vacation time saved up," I tell them.

"Perfect. Then we'll get planning," my mother says.

The server approaches our table to introduce the specials and take our drink order.

My mother orders a bottle of wine and compliments the server on her hair.

"So, business has been good?" my dad asks once we're settled.

"Really good."

I take the opportunity to show them the review the Hillards left for me.

"Aww, they consider you a part of their family now?" my mother asks. "How lovely."

I think about the endless number of calls and texts from Diane. Dare I say, I miss them a little? I don't want to jinx it though.

I sigh. "We accomplished quite a feat to get them that house."

"I guarantee no one else would've been able to do it," my father says.

I appreciate his faith in me.

"I have quite a few clients in the pipeline and should have some more closing very soon," I add.

"Of course you do," my dad exclaims. "I've always said that you could sell ice to an ice cream shop."

His silly catchphrase always makes me laugh.

"So, you said you wanted to talk to me about something?" I ask. As much as I love hearing their praise, I'm very curious about any possible hidden agenda to this dinner. And I don't mean hidden agenda in a negative way.

My parents look at each other.

"Lila," a voice shrieks.

Wait. I'd know that voice anywhere. I turn around to see the Hillards standing a few feet away, and of course they're not alone. Sara and Cal are with them.

Okay, I'm not one to believe in signs from the universe or fate or any of that stuff, but what are the chances of them coming here—tonight. It's totally my fault though. I raved to Diane about the food here on many occasions. I guess they finally decided to try it, and they happened to pick tonight. Lucky me.

My parents look over as I wave.

"Mom and Dad, these are the clients I was just telling you about, the Hillards."

Diane approaches my mother like she's a long lost friend she hasn't seen in twenty years.

"It's so good to meet you," Diane gushes.

The introductions begin, and I immediately wonder if my parents are going to recognize Cal. I should probably get out in front of any awkward moments.

"Do you guys remember Cal Sims? We went to high school together, and he's one of Theo Jorgenson's good friends," I say nonchalantly.

I can almost see the wheels turning in my mother's brain as I pray she doesn't say anything that will make everyone uncomfortable. I know she remembers him. Cal and I dated for several months, and if he wasn't at our house, he was playing basketball or hanging out at the neighbor's house.

"Urm, yes. Hello," she says slowly.

My dad shakes his hand.

"It's nice to see you both again," Cal says warmly.

"And this is his girlfriend, Sara, who's also the Hillards' niece," I add.

"Isn't this a fun coincidence?" Diane exclaims. "I had a feeling these girls were meant to meet."

One of the things working in sales has taught me is to keep a smile on my face at all costs.

Diane continues talking about getting their home, which is a better subject than how Cal and I know each other.

The host interrupts her and points to the empty table right next to us. "Would you like this table?"

"Oh, we don't want to intrude," Dave chimes in. He always seems to be the voice of reason when it comes to his wife. I've always liked Dave Hillard.

"No intrusion at all," my mother says. I notice her eyes move down to Diane's black rubber sandals. She'd never say anything to her, but I know what's she's thinking. If they were friends she'd tell Diane to burn them this instant.

Sara sits directly to my right, and motions for me to lean in with her finger.

"I'm so sorry we're interrupting your dinner."

I wave my hand. "It's fine."

Even though our tables are right next to each other, we're not actually sitting together.

The four of them start discussing the menu and talking to the server. My mom leans over to whisper to me.

"Is my memory failing me, or is that the same—"

I hold up my hand to stop her. I'm not sure Sara or the Hillards know about my history with Cal, and although it's been a long time, I don't want things to be weird around them.

"Yes," I whisper, putting my finger to my lips.

My dad raises his eyebrows and takes a sip of his wine.

"Anyway, what did you want to talk to me about? Does it have to do with the house?"

My dad puts his glass down.

"Lila, as you know the market is very good right now."

Ugh. I knew it.

"And of course, you'd be the listing agent."

"You're ready to sell the house." I spit out the words like they're poison.

"Not immediately," my mom insists. "But within the next few months we'd like to get it all wrapped up since things are going so well in your career. And we know you have roommates, so giving them notice is important."

"Why is it so urgent?" I whine.

"This is the exciting part," my dad announces.

"I've been approached by a friend to invest in a company."

I groan.

Another investment? Sometimes I wonder if it's an addiction.

"I thought you were retired and enjoying life."

"Oh, we are. I'll be completely hands-off."

What can I say? When I told them I wanted to move back into the house for a time, I knew it was on borrowed time.

"Honey, you can relax," Mom says patting my arm. "This isn't happening tomorrow, but we want you to start preparing and taking the time you need."

I nod without saying a word. I know I won't have a hard time finding a place to live, but the idea of not living with Gabby and Reagan makes me sad. Sadder than I ever expected. I'm not the one to show emotion. I usually leave that to Reagan.

I attempt to swallow the lump in my throat. "I know, it's just sad to think about saying good-bye to my childhood home."

I must say that louder than I intended because Diane hears me from their table. My parents explain that they're ready to sell the house, while I remain silent.

My gaze moves over to Cal, who gives me a comforting smile. We just had this conversation when we saw each other at the market, so I know he understands.

"Oh, Lila, just think about the fabulous home you could find yourself," Sara suggests. "That's probably a nice perk of your job."

I tighten my jaw. "Yes, you're right about that."

The subject switches back to my parents' upcoming trip, and I force myself not to think about what's to come. *It's just a house, Lila.*

After we finish dinner, we say good-bye to the Hillards, Sara, and Cal. Once we're safely outside, my mother revisits the subject of Cal.

"I haven't thought about Cal Sims in years. Didn't you two have a messy teenage breakup?"

I bite my lower lip. "Yes, that's exactly what it was."

I hold my arms out to give her a hug and then hug my father.

My mom says she will be in touch to make plans for me to join them in New York. Who knows when that will actually happen, especially now because I need to start looking for a place to live.

Ugh. The thought of it makes me nauseated.

I just have to pull myself together, because I can do this. I sell people's homes every day, so why is it bothering me so much? Now I just have to figure out the best way to break the news to my roommates that change is coming.

Chapter Seven

The big day has arrived. It's party time.

Never in all my wildest dreams did I ever think Theo's birthday would turn into such a big production and I'd be a part of it. Our house is decorated with all the party trimmings—streamers, balloons, and confetti. I actually despise confetti, but I didn't tell Gabby that. There's a DJ on the back patio, as well as loads of delicious catered food. Guests have begun to arrive, and so far I don't know a single person other than my roommates and the birthday boy. I greet a few guests and then escape out to one of the hammocks in the corner of the backyard. I can't remember the last time I sat in one, so I stretch out and stare up at the night sky. I remember when my parents had these installed. My mother was on a home renovation kick and one of her projects was the backyard. She thought of everything to enhance the area around the pool, from the outdoor kitchen to artificial turf. Her backyard design drew quite a bit of attention and was even featured in lifestyle and home decor magazines. She was over the moon, and the Barlow backyard became famous.

It's the perfect time to relax for a few minutes while the party is gearing up. My plan is go out of my way and be present for Gabby throughout the night. I haven't told my roommates about the dinner with my parents yet. I figured I'd at least get through this party before delivering the bad news.

"Lila?" Reagan calls.

"Out here," I say, holding up my hand but not moving from the hammock.

"Hey, girl," a voice says. I lift my head up to see Sara sauntering over to me. She's wearing a short, pink baby doll dress. Her blonde waves brush the tops of her shoulders.

"I was about to ask what you're doing out here, but I totally get it. This is absolutely magical."

I smile. "Thanks. I figured I'd use this time to relax for a few minutes before the rager starts."

I motion to the other hammock, inviting her to sit down.

"I was about to ask, but I didn't want to interrupt your relaxation," she says, carefully sitting down in it. Her dress is a bit short, but she carefully lies down, keeping all areas covered. "Cal is already busy with Theo and all his friends."

I tighten my jaw. I don't know if Theo keeps in touch with a lot of people from high school other than Cal, but there's a good chance I might know a few of them.

"Your house is stunning by the way," she says. "I'm sure you won't have any issues selling it."

Crap. I almost forgot that she knows about it. I hope neither she nor Cal say anything to Theo or Gabby about the impending sale.

"Probably not." I pause. "Anyway, how's good ol' Diane? I haven't heard from her lately."

She laughs. "She's fine. Definitely making herself right at home in Miami."

"I don't doubt it."

The music starts to get louder, and I hear a few cheers.

"I guess that's my cue to go be social," I say, sitting up.

"Me too. The food looks divine," she says. "And I should probably find my man."

"Good idea, save him from Theo."

She leans her head to the side. "About that—Cal told me that you and Theo don't get along."

Hmm ... I wonder if that's all he said.

"We didn't for many years. He lived right next door when we were growing up," I say, pointing to his house. "I always said he was like the annoying brother I never wanted."

"And now he's going to propose to your roommate." She freezes, and all the color drains from her face.

"Um, what?"

She covers her face with her hands. "Crap. Please don't say anything."

I'm about to ask her how she knows about this turn of events, but she starts talking before I have a chance.

"I overheard Cal talking to Theo about it on the phone, but I swore I wouldn't say anything."

Wow, Gabby is going to be ecstatic. At least I think she is. Her last engagement didn't have a happy ending, so who knows.

"Is it happening tonight?"

She shrugs. "I don't know any of the details, but now I need a drink."

As we head inside, my mind is racing with questions.

Is he planning to ask her tonight at his party? Have they discussed marriage? Is she ready to take this step with him? I know Gabby's head over heels for him, but they've been together less than a year.

When I get inside, I check my phone and find a message from my friend Paul.

Hey, stranger. It's last minute, but I'm getting the crew together for a day at sea tomorrow. You in?

That's code for a party on his family's mini-yacht.

I adore my friend Paul, but things have been a little uncomfortable since he got close to Reagan's friend Bethany. She came to stay with us a few months ago, and it was a nightmare. Anyway, she connected with Paul, and I think he still spends time with her. It's a taboo subject that neither of us brings up. I know there's a chance she'll be there, but I'm certainly not going to let that stop me. My phone buzzes again with another text.

Bring Jordan.

Ugh. I guess the news hasn't gotten to him yet. We're all in the same circle, so I figured he'd know by now.

Hey, you. I'm in, but solo.

I hit send and then start typing again.

I guess you haven't heard the news. Jordan and I are no more, but everything is fine. At a party. See you tomorrow.

News travels fast via Paul, so the rest of the social circle will know before the night is over.

I look around at the party décor. Gabby really did an amazing job. She carefully thought out the details and went with a sports theme because Theo loves everything sports related.

The guests are a wide range of ages, and everyone seems to be having a great time. The catering company sent a few people to take care of food and make sure everything is running smoothly.

Reagan and her boyfriend, Jeremy, are slow-dancing to a fast song. Those two just started dating within the last few months and are completely enamored with one another. They actually might be more outwardly affectionate than Gabby and Theo. She has her arms linked around his neck, and his are wrapped around her waist. They are gazing into each other eyes, and by the looks of it, you'd think they were the only two people at this party, or on this planet.

Gabby putters around the kitchen in her black romper and denim jacket.

"Everything is going smoothly," I reassure her.

She lets out a puff of air. "I know. I'm so relieved."

I chew on my lip. I wonder if she has any idea what could go down tonight. I'm dying to say something, but I know I can't.

"You've made this a special night, so just enjoy it."

She wanders off to mingle while I contemplate the possibilities of the night ahead. Would Theo use his own party as a place to propose? It's not the most romantic of places, but maybe he'd want to do it in front of their friends.

"Lila?"

I turn to see Cal standing next to me. He's wearing a light

blue button-down shirt and black pants. His blue eyes are sparking behind a pair of glasses.

"Oh, hey."

"You ok? You were staring off into space."

Hmm … how long has he been standing here?

"Great. Having a blast."

"That's good." He pauses and looks around the kitchen. "Wow, how long has it been since the last time I was here?"

I press my lips together. It was only a matter of time before we talked about this.

"Years. You never came back after Theo told you about Brent."

I'm not sure why I brought that up, but it's the truth.

He gives a disapproving scowl. "Oh, yeah. Whatever happened to that guy?"

I shrug. "I'm not sure. I never saw him again after that day."

For some reason I feel the need to make this point. I never cheated on Cal, and I stand by that. I know it's in the past, but sometimes those unresolved things can sit and fester.

"Lila, I'm sorry about how things ended between us. I was immature and stupid."

"You were mean," I say, folding my arms against my chest.

He looks down at the floor.

"But it was a long time ago, and I appreciate your apology," I add.

There's loud cheering coming from the backyard, but I couldn't care less. This conversation is years overdue.

"Sometimes I wish I could go back in time," Cal mumbles.

I throw my head back and sigh. "You have no idea."

We both grow quiet again.

"Does Sara know that we dated?" I ask a few seconds later.

He nods his head. "I told her, but she knows it was in high school. I didn't want it to impact you two becoming friends."

"No. Of course not."

Our eyes lock, and I quickly look away.

"The house looks great though," he says. "Are you ready to sell?"

I put my finger to my lips and look around. "Shhh. No one knows yet."

He cringes. "Sorry."

Theo and another guy I don't recognize interrupt our conversation and drag Cal away.

I exhale loudly. It definitely feels good to have that over with. At least now the awkwardness should be gone if we continue to run into each other like we have been. And it's a relief that Sara knows.

I fill a small plate with cheese and veggies and look around as I munch on a piece of celery. There are people dancing, and there's a fun and lighthearted energy in the air. Dare I say, I'm enjoying myself? All of a sudden something catches my eye.

Sara is talking to a guy with chin-length brown hair near the bar. He's very attractive in a rugged, bad boy kind of way. Something about their interaction seems odd to me. They aren't standing super close to one another, but he keeps looking around cautiously. It almost seems like he's on guard. And Sara is gazing at him like a teenager at a boy band concert. I'd know her expression anywhere. I've used that same expression on many occasions. Curiosity is taking over—so me and my plate of food casually start moving toward them.

All of a sudden the DJ stops the music and asks for everyone's attention. There's a bit of commotion, then a spotlight shines on the hammocks where Theo and Gabby are talking.

Right away I know what's happening. That's the exact place they met, and I'm betting that's where Theo's going to propose.

Reagan comes running over to me and grabs my arm. "Is this what I think it is?"

Theo takes a microphone and starts talking about how his life changed the moment he met Gabby and how she fell out of the hammock and into his heart.

That line totally makes me cringe.

Like clockwork, he gets down on one knee and produces a little white box. A collective gasp moves through the crowd as he asks her to spend the rest of her life with him. Tears start streaming down Gabby's cheeks before she yells yes. Her hand is shaking as Theo slides a ring on her outstretched finger. And just like that, my friend Gabby is engaged to my neighbor Theo.

Life is certainly full of surprises.

Chapter Eight

"This is so romantic," Reagan says, clutching her chest. I nod without saying a word, but tears have filled my eyes. Gabby has told us repeatedly that she was completely broken before moving to Miami and that Theo restored something in her she thought was lost forever.

The party guests are all charging toward the happy couple, so Reagan and I hang back to give them space. We'll have plenty of time to talk to her later tonight after everyone leaves.

"Do you think she had any idea?" Reagan wonders aloud.

"I don't think so. She looked completely shocked."

I don't tell her that Sara let it slip. It doesn't matter now anyway.

"I'm thrilled for her." She pauses. "I guess this means we won't be living together forever after all."

Hearing her say this feels like a knife going through my chest.

"At least she'll be right next door to us," Reagan adds. "Assuming they stay in Theo's house."

My mind starts spinning. She's right about us not living together, only it's not only Gabby who'll be leaving.

"What's wrong?" Reagan asks, interrupting my thoughts. "You are happy for them, aren't you?"

If she had asked me this same question a year ago, I don't know what I'd say, but things are different now.

"Of course. Gabby deserves this, and I know Theo loves her."

I'm going to have to tell Reagan and Gabby that we're selling the house. I didn't want to bring the mood down before the party, but at least Gabby's engagement should soften the blow for her.

Reagan is another story. When she first moved here she was living with her sister, Kennedy, who's fun but very intense. She was beyond thrilled to move in with me and Gabby. I keep reminding myself that we have time. My parents didn't say we had to move right away.

"Isn't this exciting?" Sara squeals as she joins Reagan and

me. I'm sure she's relieved that the cat is out of the bag after she slipped and told me what she overheard.

All of sudden, I remember her talking to that mystery man. Theo's surprise proposal interrupted their conversation before I had a chance to make it over there. I quickly look around but don't see her friend.

Reagan rushes off to find Jeremy, leaving me alone with Sara.

"Lila, I was thinking about something," she says excitedly. "I haven't mentioned it to Cal yet, but I'm sure he'll be on board. He's very supportive when it comes to my wild ideas."

A wild idea that involves Cal. This ought to be interesting.

"What's your idea?"

She clasps her hands in front of her chest. "Well, Cal and I have big plans for the future, and we've talked about getting a house."

Oh, no. Is she—

"This house is amazing. And since Theo and Gabby are getting married, we'd get to be neighbors with our close friends, which sweetens the deal even more."

Holy crap. She wants to buy my house and move into it with my ex-boyfriend. Why is that weird? It shouldn't be weird, right?

"Wow. That *is* a wild idea. Um …"

"There's so much magic and romance in the air tonight," she continues. "Don't you agree? Seeing Theo and Gabby so happy is inspiring me to begin the next phase of my life with Cal. Marriage, family, and I think this would be the perfect place to have it all."

I guess engagements can be contagious. But now's my chance to ask her about the mystery man she was talking to. I know I didn't imagine their strange vibe.

"Definitely." I look around to see if I can spot him, but I don't. He has to be a friend of Theo's or else he wouldn't be here.

"By the way, thanks for hanging with me," I say, changing the subject. "I barely know anyone at this party."

She takes a sip of her drink. "Oh, everyone is so friendly. I can introduce you around if you want."

Ah, yes. This is the perfect segue.

"Yeah, earlier I saw you talking to a guy with chin-length hair. He's definitely good-looking and hopefully single."

I'm totally going to play the single girl card to get more info. And he is attractive, so that's a bonus.

A curious look spreads across her face. "Oh, that's AJ. He's another doctor who Cal used to work with."

"Really? Tell me more," I beg.

She opens her mouth to say something, but then her face lights up as Cal approaches.

"There's my man." She wraps her arms around his neck and grips the back of his hair.

Well, that was certainly obvious. She gladly welcomed Cal's interruption. I'm usually pretty good at detecting when something seems off.

"What are you ladies gossiping about?"

I roll my eyes. "What makes you think we were gossiping?"

He laughs. "Just a wild guess."

"Lila was asking me questions about AJ," Sara tells him.

He looks surprised. "AJ, huh."

What's that supposed to mean?

"Yeah, I was curious about who he is, what he does—all the details."

"AJ is … Let's just say if you ever want to jump out of a plane or fly to Ibiza on a whim, he's your man."

Hmm … now that sounds intriguing.

"Most importantly, he's a brilliant doctor," he adds.

Sara listens intently. Maybe she's as interested in hearing more about him as I am.

"I'm always up for a vacation," I tease.

"There's Gabby," Sara squeals, interrupting our conversation.

Theo and Gabby finally break free from the crowd and are walking toward us, hand in hand. Sara goes to greet them, leaving Cal and me alone.

"Do you really want to meet AJ?" he asks.

Why does he seem so shocked by this?

"Sure, why not?" I ask.

He shoves his hands into his pockets. "AJ doesn't seem like your type."

Oh, really. Since when does Cal Sims know what my type is?

I give him a coy smile. "Ah, well I don't really have a type. I've changed a lot since we were friends."

I get the feeling that neither Sara nor Cal wants to introduce me to AJ, but for different reasons.

Our conversation ends when Gabby comes over to us. I pull her in for a massive hug.

"I'm so happy for you," I whisper. "I wanted to give you the chance to talk to the guests because I'll see you tonight."

"Thank you, Lila. This is all because of you," she says, tears filling her eyes.

Generally, I'm not much of a crier, but her teary eyes cause a bit of moisture in mine.

I pat her on the arm. "Now let me see the ring," I demand, clearing my throat.

She holds up her left hand, displaying a stunning pear-shaped diamond on a thin, diamond-encrusted band.

"Wow, Theo did good," I exclaim. "I'm super impressed and a little surprised."

She laughs. "Not as surprised as I am."

"So you had no idea this was going to happen?"

"No clue at all," she says. "We've only discussed marriage a couple of times."

A few more guests approach Gabby, so I hang back to allow her to talk.

Out of the corner of my eye, I see Cal, Sara, and AJ together. Cal and AJ are talking, and Sara is standing in between them, sipping her drink. There's something about her body language, the way she's standing and facing AJ that makes me even more curious.

I stand up straight and make my way over to join them.

"Is everyone enjoying the party?" I ask, pretending to be the best hostess ever.

AJ flashes me a brilliant smile. "It's a terrific party, and you are?"

Cal puts his hand on AJ's shoulder and sighs.

"AJ, this is Lila Barlow. She's one of the party hosts. This is her house."

AJ holds out his hand to me. "It's nice to meet you. You certainly know how to throw a party."

I shrug. "Thank you, but I can't take any of the credit. This was all Gabby."

"Well then, I'll be sure to tell her later. I think she's a little busy now."

We all glance over at Gabby, who looks happier than I've ever seen her.

"So, AJ, how do you know the birthday boy?" I ask playfully.

A little flirting never hurt anyone. And since I'm single, I've got nothing to lose.

He points to Cal. "I met Theo through this guy. Circa who knows how many years ago. It was an adventure in Cancun, and we can leave it at that."

"Whoa. That's all you're going to say?" I look at Sara. "Have you heard this story?"

She looks back and forth between the men. "Bits and pieces. But I'm sure Cal cleaned it up for me."

Cal gives an innocent shrug. "I told you everything I remember."

I laugh. "That's a fair answer."

"So, Lila, what do you do?" AJ asks, running his hand through his hair.

Full disclosure. AJ is kind of hot.

I launch into the details about my career, which is a subject that's easy to talk about.

AJ smiles. "Very impressive. I dabble in real estate here and there. My brother-in-law and I own a few properties. He manages them, and I'm just in it for the fun."

"Lila helped my aunt and uncle find their dream home," Sara chimes in. "They adore her."

I give her a warm smile. "And I them."

Diane's endless calls and texts may have gone over the top, but she's a sweet lady.

"So you just have fun and make your brother-in-law do all the work?" I ask.

AJ takes a sip of his drink. He chuckles. "Wow—we just met, and you know me so well already."

Neither Sara nor Cal seem enthused by our banter. I'm not sure why they'd care, either.

Wasn't Diane just asking Sara about Cal introducing me to one of his doctor friends?

"To answer your question, I'm an anesthesiologist," he says. "I used to work with Cal."

Cal nods. "It was always an adventure working with you, Dr. Bennett."

AJ grips his shoulder. "And you, Dr. Sims."

"So you're everyone's favorite doctor," I suggest. "Who doesn't love the anesthesiologist?"

"Exactly."

Applause suddenly erupts, making us turn around to see Gabby and Reagan bringing out a huge birthday cake. The guests start singing "Happy Birthday" to Theo. Theo wraps his arms around Gabby and kisses her. It's all very romantic and theatrical.

With the presentation of the cake, my conversation with AJ ends as the party begins to wind down.

I sit down on an outdoor couch with my phone and curl my legs under me. I watch as AJ joins Theo and a few other guys. They all hold up their drinks to toast Theo.

Off to the side, Sara and Cal are leaning into each other and neither of them looks happy. I quickly look away so they don't catch me staring. When I finally look at my phone, I have a message waiting for me from Jordan.

Paul invited me on the boat tomorrow. He told me you'd be there. I can skip if it makes you more comfortable.

I groan. I don't want him to feel like we can't be around each other, especially because we have a lot of the same friends. I send a quick reply.

No, please don't miss it because of me. See you tomorrow.

I don't mind him being there. In fact, it might make it easier if everyone sees that we're still friends. I'd rather get it out in the open, and maybe that will keep the rumors to a minimum.

∽

"Well, that party turned out to be more exciting than I expected," Reagan says, falling down on the couch next to me. All of the guests have left, and Gabby walked Theo next door.

"That's for sure. I don't think any of us expected a big public proposal," I say. Even Sara didn't know if it was happening tonight, unless she was lying about that.

Reagan starts talking about wedding plans while I'm trying to decide if it's the right time to tell her that my parents want to sell the house.

"Things with Jeremy seem to be going very well," I say. "You two are so cute."

Her face lights up like a Christmas tree. "Sometimes I can't believe that we're together."

"Well, enjoy every second of it," I say, patting her on the hand.

She gives me a curious look. "I noticed that you talked to Cal a lot tonight."

The mention of Cal reminds me how he reacted when I asked about AJ. I need to ask Gabby what she knows about him.

"A little. I guess there's a level of comfort with him because we've known each other for so long."

She nods. "I get it. Are you sure that's it?"

I hear the french door open. "Hello."

"In here," I yell.

Gabby walks in, a huge smile spread across her face.

"There's the bride-to-be," I announce.

She sits down between Reagan and me and lets out a huge sigh. She holds out her left hand and bursts into tears. And I don't think they're happy tears. Well, that definitely wasn't the reaction I was expecting.

Chapter Nine

"It's been an exciting night," Reagan says, handing Gabby a glass of water.

Gabby nods before blowing her nose into a tissue I brought her.

"I've never been so happy, scared, and overwhelmed in my life," Gabby says, her voice shaking. "I know I want to marry Theo, but I'm terrified. My last engagement was a disaster, and I'm worried I might fail again. What if I get cold feet and hurt Theo? I'll never be able to forgive myself."

"You won't, and this is completely different," I remind her. "Theo isn't that horrible Dustin."

She holds a pillow tightly to her chest. "You're right. He's nothing like Dustin."

"If there's anything I've learned, it's to be happy in every moment," I insist. "This should be the best time in your life, so embrace it and don't let the past ruin it for you."

"I agree, and it's okay to be cautious," Reagan adds. "What happened to you is traumatic, and I'm sure Theo knows that."

"He does," Gabby says. "He told me we could take our time making plans. He just wanted to publicly show me he was committed to a future with me. And he wanted to propose at the place we met."

I giggle. "Who would've guessed the hammocks in the backyard would be so special?"

"They are ... this house will always mean so much to me."

Ugh. Hearing her say that feels like a stab through my heart.

"Anyway, did you girls enjoy the party?" Gabby asks. "I'm sorry I was so preoccupied with making sure everything went smoothly, and then the proposal threw me for a loop."

"It's was a blast," Reagan says.

My mind goes back to Cal, Sara, and AJ. I'm really interested to learn more about that dynamic.

"What about you?" Gabby asks me.

"I had a good time."

She breathes a sigh of relief, almost as if everything was hanging in the balance based on my experience.

"You know I love a good party, and I met some new people—like AJ Bennett. Tell me more about him," I say.

The corner of Gabby's mouth curls up. "Why?"

"I'm just curious."

She sips her water. "I've only been around him a few times. Theo actually met him through Cal."

I nod. "Yes, I heard he and Cal used to work together."

"Which one is AJ?" Reagan asks.

The image of AJ and Sara talking pops into my head. I describe him, and her mouth drops open.

"Ohhh, I saw him."

"AJ is definitely fun," Gabby adds. "And he's always been nice to me. Theo says he's usually the life of the party."

"I can see that."

"Now tell me why you're curious," she demands.

I tighten my jaw. I want to tell them about seeing Sara talking to AJ and about how she was acting when I asked her about him.

"AJ is attractive," I say.

"And."

"I think there's something going on with him and Sara," I blurt out.

Gabby frowns.

"Cal's girlfriend, Sara?"

I hold up my hand. "Before you say anything, hear me out."

I continue to tell her about their body language and how she was clearly bothered when he and I were talking.

"I know I'm reaching here, but I usually have a sense for this stuff."

"So, you think she cheated on Cal with him?" Reagan asks.

"I didn't say that, but there's definitely some interest there."

Gabby gives me thoughtful look. "Well, there is one thing …"

Ah, I knew it.

"What?"

She goes on to tell us about a dinner she went to with Theo and his friends.

"Sara had a lot to drink, and she was being very affectionate with everyone. Cal was visibly frustrated, so AJ kind of stepped in and helped. He was very attentive, almost affectionate with her. I thought it was a little over the top, but I didn't want to say anything. It was one of the first times I met Theo's friends, so I certainly wasn't going to question anyone's behavior at that point."

"So this happened a while ago?"

"Yes."

"Sara is a nice person," she adds. "And she and Cal seem to be happy, so I don't know."

I chew on my lip while Gabby and Reagan exchange a glance. I already know what they're thinking. I'm sure it sounds like I'm making a big deal out of nothing.

"I know how this sounds," I interject. "I promise I'm not assuming things because she's Cal's girlfriend."

They don't say anything, so I continue, "AJ and I were flirting, and Sara wasn't happy about it. It was written all over her face."

Neither was Cal, but I don't tell them that.

"So, what are you going to do?" Reagan asks.

That's one of the things I love about Reagan. She's sweet and kind, but she has a feisty side to her.

"Sara and I are supposed to meet up sometime soon," I say. "I'll see if I can get any information, although she probably won't tell me. She knows that Cal and I dated, and I'm not sure how she feels about that."

"Okay, so do you want to know because you're interested in AJ or because of Cal?" Gabby asks.

I purse my lips together. Admittedly, something about AJ is very intriguing. At the same time, there will always be a place in my heart for Cal. I was hurt when things ended, but at the same time I feel a strange need to be protective of him.

"Honestly, a little of both."

Gabby shrugs. "Well, Sara and Cal seem happy, but I thought Dustin and I were happy too. And we all know what happened with that."

Gabby zones out. A wave of guilt rushes over me. This is totally her night, and we shouldn't be talking about other people's drama.

"Enough about that," I say, jumping up from the couch. "I'm going out on Paul's boat tomorrow and guess who's going."

Reagan gets a horrified look on her face. "Bethany?"

I frown. "Ew. I hope not."

Paul didn't mention Bethany, but I wouldn't be surprised if she slithers onto that boat tomorrow.

"He invited Jordan."

"Are you okay with that?" Gabby asks.

"Actually, yes. I care about Jordan, and I hope that we can be friends after the dust settles. He's one of the best guys I know."

As we continue talking, we drag ourselves off the couch and start cleaning up. In the back of my mind, I keep thinking about selling this house and how much I'm going to miss these late night chats with my roommates.

I love Miami. Honestly, I don't know if I could live anywhere else. People always seem surprised when I tell them I've lived in the same place all of my life. Our city has so much culture, nightlife, and beauty. It's a gorgeous morning, and even though I stayed up way too late, I'm full of energy. There's something so invigorating about spending the day on the water. Paul and I have been friends for years, only I haven't seen him in several months. I'm not too concerned about it though, because we always pick up right where we left off—even if we're mad at each other. I actually don't think anything can upset me today, not even seeing Jordan. I just want to have fun and not worry about men, relationships, or selling my house.

"Lila Barlow has arrived," Paul announces dramatically. He's wearing a white button-down shirt, hot pink shorts and a captain's hat.

"Nice hat," I tease. "I'm surprised it took you so long to get one of those."

"I thought the same thing," he says. "It suits me, don't you think?"

I laugh. "I actually think that hat was made especially for you."

He does a little bow.

"More importantly, how are you doing?" he asks, concern in his voice.

I know he's talking about Jordan.

"I'm totally fine."

He grits his teeth. "Jordan might be coming today. I hope it won't make things more difficult."

I shake my head. "Nope. He sent me a text last night. It's all good."

He breathes a sigh of relief. Paul takes his parties very seriously. I know he doesn't want to deal with any drama. If only he recognized that his good buddy Bethany always brings a good dose of drama.

A few other people join us, so I move on to make my rounds, saying hello to everyone and stopping by the smoothie bar to get a green juice. I love that Paul starts off his parties with a juice bar. Some people are able to drink alcohol first thing in the morning, and it baffles me. I wander up to the upper deck, and as soon as I turn a corner I come face to face with one of the worst people I've ever met. Bethany.

I knew there was a chance she'd be here today, but I was secretly praying something else would've come up. Work, a nasty stomach bug, chicken pox, anything.

"Oh, hello, Bethany," I mutter through a forced smile. She's wearing a tight, white, knit dress, that's almost see-through. It's actually an improvement compared to other outfits I've seen her wear. She also has one of the worst spray tans I've ever seen. Her feet and hands are orange and splotchy.

"Lila, it's so nice of you to join us today."

Ugh. She's so irritating. This isn't her boat, whether she likes it or not.

"You too," I reply. "How are you?"

Ugh. Why did I even ask her that question? I couldn't care less about how she is.

"I'm wonderful. I'm loving my job and getting to know my new home. I was made to live in this city."

Ugh. Poor Miami. When Bethany came to visit Reagan, she suddenly decided she wanted to move here from Illinois. Reagan didn't think she would go through with it, but here we are.

"Good for you."

"How's Reagan doing?"

Like she actually cares. She set out to sabotage her all while she was staying under our roof.

"Happy and content," I reply. Sometimes this is the best payback when someone tries to inflict misery on a person.

"I'm glad to hear it," she says. "I've been meaning to reach out to her."

Why on earth would she do that? I desperately want to ask her this question, but I hold back because she probably won't contact her anyway. And I certainly don't want to encourage her to do so.

"Did you hear that Dante is opening a second restaurant?" she asks. "He's doing so well."

Dante is Reagan and Bethany's friend from college. Reagan was hung up on him for years and just when it looked like they finally had their chance Bethany barged in and messed it up. It actually worked out in Reagan's favor though, because Jeremy is a much better man for her. Dante's first priority is his restaurant, and Reagan deserves more.

"I think I heard something about it," I say, looking around for an excuse to escape this conversation.

Like clockwork, Jordan comes up the stairs. He really does have perfect timing. I'd rather talk to the man I just broke up with than with this woman.

"Bethany, if you'll excuse me, I have to talk to a friend of mine."

I walk away before she has a chance to respond.

"Hey," I say cautiously.

A smile spreads across his face. "Hi, yourself."

Jordan is so handsome. And for a tiny instant I wonder if I made a mistake. I'll probably feel this way every time I see him, at least for a while.

"It's a beautiful day."

He laughs. "Yes, it is. I guess this is how our conversations will go now? Talking about the weather."

I giggle. "Probably."

We chat for a few minutes, and I tell him about Gabby's engagement.

"Oh, wow. Tell her I said congratulations." He pauses. "That was fast."

"Tell me about it," I agree. "But she's happy, and that's what matters."

He nods. "Exactly."

I'm not sure if we're still talking about Gabby or about me. Either way, I'm glad we're talking, and I'm hopeful that this is a sign for the future.

Chapter Ten

After Jordan and I go our separate ways to mingle, the captain announces that we will be setting sail in a few minutes. I'm usually right in the middle of all the action at these parties, but today I park myself in a cozy lounge chair on the top deck. I sip on my green drink and look out over the bay. There's a light breeze, which cools my skin in contrast to the warm sun. I put my sunglasses on and close my eyes for a few seconds.

"Hey, again."

I cringe at the sound of Bethany's voice. I'd rather spend hours locked in a room with people scratching their fingernails down chalkboards.

She obviously doesn't pick up on my disinterest in talking to her and sits on the chair across from me. I'm not sure why she's following me around, but I'll lose my mind if this continues all day. I guess throwing myself overboard is always an option. There's not much of a difference between her and the sharks in the water.

"Hey," I reply, not looking at her. Maybe she'll get the hint if I don't pay her much attention.

"So, I was talking to Paul the other day about something that's weighing on my heart, and he suggested I ask you."

I tighten my jaw. Paul is totally on my list right now.

"I know we've had a few tiny issues, but we're adults, so I know we can get past them for Reagan's sake."

Tiny issues? Bethany is as delusional as ever. At the same time I'm actually curious as to what she wants to talk to me about.

I turn my head to face her. "What do you want to ask me?"

She pushes her hair behind her shoulder and lets out a dramatic sigh.

"Reagan really hurt me deeply when she kicked me out on the street," she says sadly, her face falling. "I thought I'd never forgive her, but lately I've been thinking about it. Maybe it's time we all move on and start anew."

It's taking all my strength not to laugh right now. First of all, Reagan has nothing to be forgiven for. Bethany came to town to get back at Reagan for leaving her behind in Chicago. She resented her for starting a new life and finding happiness. According to Reagan, Bethany doesn't have family, so she expected Reagan to fill that deep void and always be there.

"I'm not sure why you're talking to me about this," I say. "Your issues with Reagan don't have anything to do with me."

I actually sensed Bethany was trouble from the moment she stepped into my house, but I let Reagan figure it out for herself. My friend is better off without her in her life.

"You're her roommate. She'll listen to you."

Basically she's asking me to help fix her friendship with Reagan. Clearly she doesn't know me at all.

"I'm sorry, but I can't help you," I say flatly.

She frowns. "You don't know Reagan like I do," she snaps. "She doesn't like being at odds with her friends—or anyone. It will eat away at her."

I shrug. "It's still none of my business."

Bethany folds her arms against her chest. Her legs are bouncing quickly. "Fine."

She doesn't say anything but doesn't leave either. I guess that's the end of my quiet time. I start to sit up.

"I'm not as bad as you think I am," she exclaims, rising to her feet.

Ugh. I really don't care.

"Look, Bethany, if you want to try to reach out to Reagan, that's up to you, but I'm staying out of it."

I walk away from her without giving her a chance to respond. I suppose it's better than jumping overboard.

~

Maybe I should buy a boat? I think about his every time I come to one of these parties. Of course any boat I could afford wouldn't be a mini-yacht like this one. Other than that annoying Bethany, I'm having a lovely time. I've been able to catch up with several friends, and the brunch spread is fabulous. My lack of cooking skills makes me really appreciate good food when I go to events. Paul, our friend Harry, and I are sitting out on the deck when I tell them about my parents' decision to finally sell the house.

"That's sad. It's like the end of an era," Harry says dramatically.

"Hah! You're telling me. I never thought it would be so hard for me."

"Yeah, what's up with you having all these emotions? Aren't you supposed to be dead inside?" Harry teases.

I giggle. "Mostly."

"Could you buy the house?" Paul asks. "I'm sure your parents would cut you a deal."

I shrug. "I've thought about it, but the realtor in me doesn't want to do that to my clients. I know what that house is worth, and it might be a bit steep for my first home. My parents deserve to get top dollar for their investment."

Paul nods. "Good point."

"I haven't told Reagan and Gabby yet," I continue. "I think that's one of the things I'm the saddest about."

"You guys could always find another place together," Paul suggests.

"You're right ... But things are about to change anyway. Gabby's engaged now—so she'd be moving out at some point."

"And what about Jordan?" Harry asks. "Now that you're available again, does this mean you're ready to give us another shot?"

I laugh and put my hand on his cheek.

"Baby, you and I are like fire and ice."

Harry and I dated for a few weeks. He's a lot of fun, but we quickly learned that we're not compatible.

"True, but I'm all about living on the edge."

Paul makes a face. "Dude, you've been down that road. You're asking for trouble."

"Speaking of trouble," I exclaim, "what's up with you

suggesting that Bethany talk to me? I was ready to throw myself overboard earlier."

He cringes. "Yeah, I instantly regretted that after she talked to me."

"I still can't believe you haven't kicked her to the curb yet," I say, shaking my head.

"She's actually not that bad," Paul insists.

Harry makes a face. "That's what you want to believe. She already told you she wasn't interested in you as more than a friend—give up the dream."

"Yes, give it up," I chime in.

Our conversation is interrupted when one of the crew approaches us.

"You sure you're okay?" Harry asks after Paul leaves.

I nod. "Yes, there's just been a lot going on. Nothing I can't handle though."

"Of course not. Lila Barlow can handle anything."

I smile. "I appreciate your faith in me."

He looks behind me and frowns. "I definitely agree with you about her."

I turn around to see Bethany with her arms around Paul's and Jordan's shoulders. The sight causes a surge of adrenaline to shoot through my body. As bad as I want to jump in and save the day by getting her yucky arm off

Jordan, I can't. It was my decision to end our relationship, so he has the freedom to talk to anyone. Even Bethany. Ugh, the thought makes me want to puke.

"Does that make you fired up?" Harry asks, a mischievous grin on his face. "Seeing her hands all over your ex-boyfriend?"

"You'd love to see that wouldn't you?"

"Hell, yes. I love when feisty Lila comes out. She turns me on."

I shake my head. "You're bad."

He leans into me. "Come on, admit that you're finally ready to settle down with me. We'd have some gorgeous children."

I wrap my arm around Harry's shoulders. He's really adorable with his warm, brown eyes and irresistible dimples. "Our children would be precious, but think of all the issues they'd have with us as parents. It just wouldn't be fair to them."

He nods knowingly. "That's true. So, how about we make one of those deals that if neither of us is married by the time we turn thirty-five, we get married."

"You're saying we should be each other's backups," I reiterate.

"That's exactly what I'm saying."

Hmm ... at the rate I'm going, it may not be a bad idea.

Harry and I could be life companions and travel the world together in our old age.

"Fine," I say in agreement.

Harry's eyes light up. "Really?"

I laugh. "Why not? Although, I'm sure some lucky girl will snag you before then. Who could resist those dimples?"

"You could," he reminds me.

I give him a coy smile. "You know that's not true."

I look over to see Bethany flipping her hair and batting her eyes at Jordan. She really is one of the worst people ever. At least Jordan knows what he's dealing with because we were together when she was wreaking havoc on our household.

"Don't worry. I'm sure Jordan won't be deceived by Bethany's charm," Harry says.

"I'm not worried about it."

When I get home, neither Reagan nor Gabby are there. The house is quiet, and it makes me instantly feel sad. I look around my house, and a wave of emotion comes over me. Things are changing so fast, and I better get used to it. When I made the decision to move back in here, I didn't know what to expect, but now I know it was meant to be. Becoming friends with Gabby and Reagan made it all worth it. I don't know what lies ahead, but Harry was right—I can handle anything. I'm always up for a new adventure, and I have a feeling that's exactly what I'm in for.

Chapter Eleven

"I've never seen Elizabeth so frazzled," Javier whispers. "She looks like she hasn't slept in days."

Elizabeth does look disheveled. Her hair is flat, her blouse is wrinkled, and she has dark circles under her eyes. Nothing like the powerhouse boss we're used to seeing.

Gabby asked her sister-in-law, Nikki, if anything was going on with Elizabeth, and she didn't know. Or at least that's what she said. Regardless, there has to be something because she doesn't seem like herself. And I totally get it. Sometimes life throws weird curveballs our way, and we have to figure out how to handle them.

"I'll talk to her today," I reply.

Suzanna is typing away on her laptop, but I know she's trying to listen to our conversation.

When Gabby arrives, the whole office is abuzz with her engagement news. I've never seen her so happy, and it could be my imagination, but I feel like she's more focused on her work this morning. One of her clients finally put in an offer on a home after dragging their feet for a month. I'm thrilled for her, because she really needed a few wins.

I'm listening to Gabby tell Javier about Theo's party when my phone rings. I'm surprised to see Sara's number on the screen, and I hesitate for a few seconds before finally answering.

"This is Lila Barlow."

"Hey, girl, it's Sara. I have the best news."

My ears perk up. Who doesn't love *the best* news?

"Do tell."

"Cal and I were talking, and I think I finally convinced him that we should buy your house."

What?

I frown. First of all the house isn't even for sale yet. And how can they decide this already, not even knowing what we're listing it for? I've pulled the specs, but I've been avoiding them—pictures haven't been taken yet, and I haven't even told my roommates.

I glance over at Gabby, who's scrolling through her phone, showing Javier pictures from the party. This isn't the place I want to break the news to her.

"That's great. I'll let you know as soon as it's listed, and we can go from there."

"Oh, I was thinking you wouldn't even have to list it," she suggests. "We could meet up for dinner and work out all the details."

Damn, she's pushy.

"That's a possibility we can discuss for sure."

I'm trying to sound professional and satisfy her at the same time. I have a feeling I'm about to have a Diane, Part Two on my hands. Endless calls and texts—just when I thought I was free.

"Anyway, we can talk about that later," she says. "The other reason I'm calling is to invite you to a birthday lunch for Aunt Diane."

She goes on to give me the details, and I add it to my schedule. Since I have Sara on the phone and Gabby is now busy with her own phone call, I take the chance to ask her about AJ. I'm not surprised when she grows quiet.

"Um, sure. I can ask Cal for his info."

"That would be amazing," I say. "Things got so crazy at the party that I didn't have a chance to talk to him again."

My intuition is kicked into overdrive. Sara doesn't want me to reach out to AJ, and I'm going to find out why. When we get off the phone, I wait for Gabby to finish her call and then tell her about my theory.

"I'm sure Theo can connect you with AJ."

I nod. "I know. But I don't understand why Sara is acting so strange about it."

Gabby presses her lips together but doesn't say anything.

"In other news, guess who I had the pleasure of seeing on Paul's boat?"

I haven't had a chance to talk to her or Reagan about Bethany yet.

"Jordan?"

"Well, yes. But that was fine. Bethany was there, and she wants me to talk to Reagan for her."

Gabby groans. "About what? I hope you set her straight."

"Ha. I tried to, but I still don't think she gets it. She still believes everything that happened was Reagan's fault and that Reagan kicked her out on the street."

"So if everything was Reagan's fault, then why does she want to talk to her?"

I shake my head. "Good question. She rambled on about deciding to forgive her after thinking she never would. It was all very dramatic, of course."

"What are you going to tell Reagan?"

"Don't you mean warn her?" I ask with a giggle.

"That too."

"I'll deliver the message and let Reagan decide what she wants to do."

I return to my desk and attempt to do some work, but I'm distracted today. I feel like there is so much happening all at once, and I can't seem to get any of it under control. I decide to abandon work for a few minutes and talk to Elizabeth.

I knock on her door and peek in her office.

"Hey, come on in," she says, putting her phone down.

I'm still so taken aback by her appearance. She obviously put forth the effort, but you can just tell when someone is struggling. Her blonde hair is pulled back into a ponytail, and she has minimal makeup compared to her usual fresh-faced self.

I sit in one of the chairs across from her desk and give her a funny look.

"What's up?" she asks.

"I was about to ask you the same thing."

She sighs. "I'm sorry if I seem preoccupied lately. I've had a lot on my plate."

"Anything I can help with?"

She hesitates and then finally starts talking. "I might have to sell or close Fun in the Sun Realty."

What? I certainly wasn't expecting her to say that. I guess that explains the comment she made about me taking over the agency.

"Why?" I ask.

"Billy was offered a promotion with his job. It's in London and an amazing opportunity for him. We've had so many late night discussions trying to figure out how we could make things work. He doesn't want to go without me, and I don't want him to miss out on anything. We're at such a stalemate, and I don't know where to go next."

Billy is Elizabeth's longtime boyfriend. I think they might be common law married or whatever it's called. I don't know how that works, but I know they almost got married in Vegas on several different occasions. They backed out at the last second because they thought they wanted a traditional wedding someday. Obviously it's never happened.

"I've always wanted to live abroad, so there's a part of me that's really excited to go," she continues.

"Can you do both?" I ask. "Maybe you could keep the agency and work remotely?"

I have no idea if this could work, but I'm trying to help.

"Trust me, I've thought about it," she says. "But you know me. As long as this place is mine, I'll never be able to step away completely. And being so far away will make it even harder. So, I probably have to make a clean break."

My brain is spinning. I've been working for Elizabeth for years, and although I could easily get another job, Fun in the Sun Realty is my home. Well, my second home. My first home is about to be sold too. The thought turns my stomach.

"I need to make an announcement soon," she says. "Could you keep this to yourself for a day or two?"

I nod. Ugh. Another secret to keep from Gabby. I'm the worst friend.

"Does Gabby know anything about this?"

She shakes her head. "That's another dilemma. I haven't even told my sister yet, and I really hate keeping things from her."

I know how she feels. I haven't even told my roommates that they need to find a new place to live. Maybe I'm afraid that if I say it out loud, I'll have to face it. And to make matters worse, I have Sara and Cal wanting to buy my house.

"That's another reason I don't want you to tell anyone yet," she begs. "I don't want Gabby to say anything to Nikki before I do."

I promise to keep it quiet and leave her to sort out her major life decisions.

"What did she say?" Javier asks as soon as I return to my desk. Gabby joins him, and I put on my best poker face.

"Not much other than she hasn't been sleeping great," I tell them.

"Uh-uh. There's more going on with her," Javier insists.

"Maybe she's just having a bad day," I suggest.

"Nope. I think there's trouble in paradise. It's something between sweet Billy boy and her."

He's on the right track—sort of. I chuckle at his Billy boy reference. Elizabeth's boyfriend is one of the nicest guys I've ever met—almost too nice.

"Maybe. But I'm certainly not one to judge or make assumptions about anyone's relationship drama."

Gabby makes a face. "Neither am I."

Thankfully, both of them return to their desks, leaving me to think about Elizabeth's news. I glance around the office, and another feeling of sadness comes over me. First my home and now this, it's almost too much to think about all at once.

～

I decide to skip Pilates class and go straight home after work. Some days it's just nice to sit in front of the TV and relax, which is something I rarely do. When I pull into the driveway, I see Theo in front of his house. He waves and starts walking towards my car, which causes a strange feeling to come over me.

I get out of the car and say hi.

"Hey. Do you have a few minutes to talk?"

For some reason my curiosity is piqued. It's not often that Theo wants to talk to me when Gabby isn't around.

"Sure. Do you want to come inside?"

Theo follows me into the house, and I offer him a drink.

"What did you want to talk about?"

"Well, first off, I wanted to thank you for such a great birthday party."

I hold up my hand and remind him that Gabby was one hundred percent behind that party. She put everything into making it perfect.

"I know, but you helped, and you've been such a great friend to her."

I open a Diet Coke and lean against the counter.

"Well, Gabby is a great friend to me too. I'm glad she's found happiness."

"Even if it means she's marrying me?" he teases.

I laugh. "Shocking, isn't it?"

We both grow quiet for a few minutes. And he looks around the house.

"Lila, I know that your parents are finally selling."

Crap. I should've known he'd find out.

"Did Cal tell you?"

He shakes his head. "It was Sara actually. She let it slip while I was talking to Cal."

Sara again, huh? She certainly has loose lips. She also let it slip that Theo was planning to propose, but I don't tell him this.

"Did you say anything to Gabby?"

He shakes his head. "It's not my place. And I learned a long time to stay out of your business."

Huh, if only he'd done that all those years ago.

"Thanks. I'm going to tell them, but with the party and everything I was just waiting for the right time."

"It's going to be a sad day when the Barlows no longer own this house."

This reminds me of Sara's phone call from earlier.

"Well, you may really like your new neighbors. Sara told me that she and Cal are interested in buying it."

Theo furrows his brow. "What?"

Oops. Did I say too much? I guess I can accidentally let things slip too.

"Oh, I guess you haven't talked to Cal since they had that conversation," I say with a shrug.

It's very possible that he didn't tell Theo. Do guys tell their friends everything like women do? I didn't think so.

"I talked to him about an hour ago. And there's no way Cal would ever buy your house."

He seems pretty adamant about it, which stirs my curiosity once again.

"Sara seemed pretty confident," I tell him. "She even suggested I don't list it and make a deal with them directly."

Theo looks confused.

"There's no way they're buying a house, especially because they've been having some issues."

My ears perk up, and Theo makes a face. I might as well use this time to ask him about AJ. What the hell, I have nothing to lose at this point.

"Do their issues have anything to do with AJ?"

"AJ Bennett?" he asks.

"That's the one."

I can almost see the wheels turning in Theo's head.

"Do you know something I should?"

I sigh. "I don't know anything, but I know what I saw at the party. And whenever I ask her about him, she gets really uncomfortable and jittery."

Theo frowns. "What did you see?"

I tell him about watching them together and their body language.

"So they didn't do anything?"

"No … You don't believe it, do you?"

He holds up his hand. "I didn't say that. And AJ is—well, he's not someone who likes to be tied down."

"Cal seemed surprised when I asked about AJ too," I tell him.

Theo is quiet.

I get the feeling that I'm missing something here. Why would Sara tell me they wanted to buy the house, yet Theo says that there's no way they would? And what's the deal with this AJ guy?

"I'm confused. Isn't AJ your friend?"

"Yes. I mean we're not besties or anything," he says, making quotation makes with his fingers. "He's that friend that you go out with and have a few beers, but I'm not sure I'd trust him around my girlfriend."

Ah, so the truth comes out.

"So let me ask you, Theo—do you think it's possible that something has or could happen between him and Sara?"

What am I doing? Is this any of my business? Why do I even care? Theo is going to ask me this and it'll probably get back to Cal. I'm not at a place in my life where I want to be dragged back into Cal Sims's orbit. But somehow here I am.

"I don't know Sara that well," I admit.

"She's a nice person, and she and Cal have been together for about three years," he says. "Between you and me, I expected them to be engaged by now. Cal has always said that when the timing was right, he would propose, but he never has. He did tell me recently that things weren't great, but maybe they're working it out."

"Maybe by moving in together?" I suggest.

"Possibly, but they wouldn't live here."

We hear the door open, and Reagan walks in. She looks back and forth between Theo and me.

"Oh no, what's wrong?"

I giggle. "Nothing, we're just talking."

She puts her bag on the counter and says hi to Theo.

"How was your day?" I ask.

She shrugs. "It was—long. I need to go to bed early tonight."

Theo stands up. "I should get home and pack. I'm leaving early in the morning for a trip. Make sure you take care of my fiancée for me."

"We will," Reagan says.

"Thanks for talking, Lila."

"Sure, and think about what I said."

He nods. "I will."

After he leaves, I field a bunch of questions from Reagan, so I fill her in on my thoughts about Sara and AJ, leaving out the part about her and Cal moving in here.

"Promise you won't get mad at me—" she says cautiously.

"Then don't say anything to make me mad."

"After seeing Cal again, are any of those old feelings resurfacing? … I'm not judging—because I understand that more than anyone."

I sigh. "Honestly, I don't know. Maybe a few, but I also just ended things with Jordan."

This reminds me of seeing Bethany on Paul's boat.

"Ah … speaking of Jordan. I saw him yesterday."

"Oh, how was that?"

I shrug. "It actually wasn't that bad. At least not compared to seeing other people."

She grits her teeth. "Bethany?"

I nod. "You guessed it. And she really wanted to talk to me."

"About what?"

"You."

Reagan's frowns. "What about me?"

I tell her what Bethany said, and she sighs. "I feel like no matter what I do, I can't escape her."

"Of course you can," I tell her. "Don't let her manipulate you into feeling sorry for her."

She folds her hands and places them on the counter.

"I'm trying not to, but I know the only reason she acts out is for attention. I think she's just incredibly lonely."

"And that's exactly what she's hoping you'll say," I tell her.

Reagan is a much better person that I am. I hate to see her being walked all over, but she can make her own decisions. And if she chooses to bring Bethany back into her life, that's on her.

"I know. Kennedy would lose her mind if I started talking to Bethany again."

I laugh at the thought. Reagan's sister and I have similar personalities, and I think she's great, naturally.

The subject changes from Bethany back to my conversation with Theo. I'm absolutely exhausted by the time I crawl into bed. Between Elizabeth's news and Sara and Cal, I've had enough heavy stuff for one day.

Chapter Twelve

I stretch out on my mat and close my eyes. My favorite part of Pilates is those last few minutes after you've moved your body and you allow it to rest. It's been a few uneventful days since I talked to Elizabeth, and she sent out a message that she wanted to have an office meeting this morning. She sent me a separate message about meeting with me beforehand. Both Gabby and Javier have been texting me nonstop, and luckily my Pilates class was the perfect excuse to avoid their questions.

I take a quick shower and put on a denim jumpsuit. Everyone says it looks like something out of *Mamma Mia*, and I'm okay with that. I quickly blow dry my hair and let it fall naturally over my shoulders. As I'm getting ready, I think about how relaxed the environment at Fun in the Sun is. The idea of transferring to a different agency makes me nauseated. On a good note, I have a lot of connections in the industry and I know I could easily switch, but that doesn't mean I'll like it.

I give Gabby a heads up that I'm leaving for the office early, and she asks me if I know what's happening.

"I'm not sure."

And it's true. The last time I talked to Elizabeth she hadn't decided on what she was going to do.

"Do you think she's closing the agency?" she asks. "I talked to Nikki, and she mentioned something about her making some huge, life-changing decisions."

I frown. "I don't know."

She looks at her engagement ring. "Is it just me, or does everything feel like it's changing? Not all bad changes, obviously."

"Yeah, obviously," I echo. "Anyway, I'll see you at the office. We can talk more later."

When I arrive, I'm surprised to see to see Elizabeth in one of her black power suits and a pair of black stilettos. Her hair is styled, and she actually looks like her old self. I guess whatever decision she's made has brought her back to the land of the living.

"You look much better," I tell her.

"Yeah, stressed and worried isn't a good look for me," she says with a wink.

I sit down in her office and cross my legs.

"Well, what's the verdict?" I ask.

She leans back in her chair.

"I wanted you to come in early so I could talk to you about an idea I had."

I chew on my lower lip. "Okay."

"I've decided to go to London with Billy," she says cautiously.

I nod. "I had a feeling."

She tells me about how she spent many nights weighing all her options and about how she thought of every possibility and offered to show me some spreadsheets.

"Which brings me to now—I won't be here to run Fun in the Sun, but you will be. ... Would you consider taking over the agency? We could work out some sort of a deal for you, or we could partner for a while and see how things go."

There are hundreds of thoughts swirling through my mind right now.

"You don't have to decide right this second, but I hope you'll consider it. I think the others would love to stay, and you've been number one around here for a while. I believe you can take us to the next level."

Wow, it definitely makes me feel good knowing that she has so much faith in me. At the same time, I'm just not sure I want to take over the day to day operations. I love my work and the freedom it gives me.

"I'm really flattered, but I'm not sure I'm ready for that. And I'm sure Suzanna won't enjoy working for me."

She laughs. "Yeah, I thought about that. Will you at least think about it?"

I nod. "I will."

"Anyway, I'm going to update everyone today about the possibility of me going to London. And I've already reached out to a few friends, and you all would be welcomed at any of those agencies. I'd much rather the team hear from me than from someone else in the industry. I owe them that much."

I should've known Elizabeth would cover everything. Working for her has been a dream, and this news is quite a blow.

Elizabeth takes a phone call, so I return to my desk. Gabby is the first to arrive.

"What's going on?" she whispers.

I open my mouth to say something when Suzanna comes in.

"I'll text you."

Gabby heads to her desk. When I go to pick up my phone, I have a text waiting from a number I don't recognize.

Hey, it's Cal. Just got off the phone with Theo. Can we talk today if you have a few minutes?

My heart begins to pound against the walls of my chest. Did Theo tell him what I said about Sara and AJ? Ugh, I immediately regret my newfound friendship with my neighbor. We've gone this long barely being able to tolerate each other, and I throw all caution to the wind with one conversation.

Sure. I have a busy day. How about this evening?

Oh well, what's a little more added stress to my day. But, like my friend Harry said, I can handle anything.

A text from Gabby pops up on my phone.

Well?

Crap, seeing the text from Cal made me forget to text her.

Elizabeth is going to London, I type quickly.

First she gives me a curious look, and then her eyes grow wide. She doesn't have a chance to text me back before Javier arrives.

As soon as the Fun in the Sun Realty team is assembled and present in our small conference room, Elizabeth clears her throat and starts talking.

"I'm sure you've all noticed things have been a little off with me over the past month or so."

"Have we ever," Javier chimes in. "But you're looking fabulous today."

He always knows the right things to say.

She continues and gently breaks the news of her impending move to London. There's a collective gasp, and even I join in. Although I already know what's happening, it sounds as dramatic as it did when she told me.

"You're leaving?" Javier wails.

"I had a feeling," Suzanna says glumly.

"What does this mean for us?" Gabby asks.

Poor Elizabeth tries to answer questions and contain her emotions at the same time.

Gabby looks at me, and I just give her a subtle nod.

Elizabeth continues telling the team that she's looking into a few different possibilities to keep the agency open, but things are still up in the air. Thankfully she doesn't tell them about asking me to take over. The last thing I need is added pressure from Gabby and Javier. I don't think Suzanna would care either way. She's probably already prepared to move on anyway.

"I've spoken to other agencies, and there are many doors open to any of you who are willing to move over. I know this is difficult news, and I promise that I'm not making these decisions lightly"—she pauses, dabbing the corners of her eyes with a tissue—"You're all like family to me, and I've wrestled with this for days."

I find myself getting emotional as well. Fun in the Sun has been one of the constants in my life. When my relationships didn't work out, I always had my work to fall back on. I know I'll be able to move over to another agency, but I doubt anything will be like the environment here. This agency truly lives up to its name. Unfortunately, I'm still not sure I can assume the role of running it. I have a lot to think about.

∽

Anticipation can be a strange feeling. You can be super excited about something or dread it. I'm not sure what to think about my conversation with Cal. I hope Theo wouldn't throw me under the bus. Our relationship has come such a long way.

Gabby finally calmed down after Elizabeth's announcement, and luckily she had a few house showings, so she left the office early. I'm sure she'll want to talk tonight. I also need to tell her and Reagan about the house. Too many people know now, and it's going to come out. Of course I'd rather them hear it from me.

As I drive home, I realize that I haven't heard from Diane in a while, not that I'm complaining. I'm sure she's busy getting used to her new home. If it turns out that Sara and AJ have been involved, then that could potentially affect my relationship with the Hillards. Thankfully, we already closed. I'm sure they'll be Team Sara, and I'll most likely be Team Cal.

I know I'm getting way ahead of myself, but this is how my brain works. When I sort things out in my head, I'm able to see things clearly.

Just as I pull through the gates of my neighborhood, my phone rings, and I see Cal's number. I take a few deep breaths and exhale loudly. No matter what this conversation brings, I stand by everything I've said.

"Hello."

"Hey, Lila."

"Cal."

Why am I being so formal? Ugh. And why do I care so much? It's been almost ten years, and somehow Cal Sims still has some effect on me.

"How was your day?" he asks.

"Well, dear," I say sarcastically, which makes him laugh. "It was actually pretty stressful. We have some big changes happening, so everything feels chaotic. How about you?"

"I'm working the evening shift tonight, so I'm getting ready to go in."

"Ah, yes. Dr. Sims."

I'm actually not surprised that Cal became a doctor because he's always had a nurturing quality. I remember a time there was a car accident right in front of our high school. Cal was the first person to jump in and help. He had an amazing bedside manner even at the age of eighteen, so I'm sure it's even better now. That day when Gabby first moved in, I never expected *he'd* be the doctor she saw after falling out of the hammock. I was so surprised to hear that my new roommate was hanging out with both Theo and Cal.

"Anyway, I'm sure you want to unwind after your day, so I won't keep you long."

"It's fine," I say quickly.

He launches into his conversation with Theo. Thankfully there's no mention of AJ. At least not yet.

"Just to be clear, Sara and I did have a discussion about buying your house. But that's all it was."

"Well, she made it sound like a done deal," I tell him. "She even told me not to list it."

He sighs. "I'm sorry. Sara can be overzealous at times. Once she gets something in her head, that's all she can think about."

Hmm ... like AJ?

"It's okay ... She really must like the house. I mean, she mentioned that you two have been talking about moving in together."

"We have—off and on."

"And I'm sure you'd love to be right next door to your bestie."

He chuckles. "Yes, that would be great. But it wouldn't feel right living in your house. There are too many memories."

Memories? Does he mean—of *us*?

"Well, yes, but that was a long time ago."

He doesn't say anything, and my pulse begins to pick up.

I clear my throat. "So, I guess you'll have to talk Sara out of it."

"Um, yeah. I'm counting on you to get it sold before she even realizes it."

"I'll do my best," I say. "We're not in a rush, but I need to start the process soon. Doing projects and touchups around the house and stuff like that."

We chat for a few more minutes, and I realize how nice and comfortable this feels. Thankfully, Theo didn't let me down and there's no mention of AJ. I'm not trying to cause trouble, and it's not like I actually want his girlfriend to cheat on him. When we finally get off the phone, I stare at the screen for a few minutes as I try to make sense of what I'm feeling. Is there actually a part of me that wants something to be going on with Sara and AJ? That would make me a terrible person, right? Ugh. The good news is that Cal won't be living in my home with his future wife.

Chapter Thirteen

I never thought I'd be going to a birthday lunch for Diane Hillard, but a lot of aspects of my life don't make much sense right now. I considered canceling but I really do like Diane. She's a good person, and today is about her.

When I arrive at the Serena Rooftop, I immediately see that Sara went all out for this celebration. I have a feeling she doesn't do anything small, which I guess is one of the traits that Diane recognized in both of us.

There are two bunches of pink and green balloons. A large vase with pink and white flowers sits in the center of the table, and a gorgeous cake with pink and gold embellishments. There's even a small bottle of Mountain Dew wrapped with a bow at each seat. Clever.

I notice a stack of gifts, so I add the card I brought to the pile. Sara and an older woman who looks just like her are talking to an elegant redheaded woman by the bar.

"Lila, you made it," Sara exclaims. She seems surprised to see me. Why does everyone have the same reaction when I actually show up to these parties?

"Love the outfit," she says with a smirk.

Of course she and I are both wearing shift dresses and booties.

"I love yours too."

"Mom, this is Lila Barlow," Sara says. "She's Aunt Diane's relator."

"Oh, yes. Diane hasn't stopped talking about you," she gushes. "And you're as gorgeous as she said you were."

Out of the corner of my eye, I think I see Sara scowl, unless my eyes are playing tricks on me.

"And you're Christine, Diane's best friend. It's a pleasure."

Her eyes light up. "In the flesh."

She introduces me to the redhead, who's another friend of hers and Diane's. Both ladies are wearing pastel floral print dresses and have the same shoulder-length bob hairstyle.

Two other women arrive and place their gifts on the already towering pile. I think I recognize them from the Hillards' housewarming party, although that night is still a bit of a blur. I'm really happy for Diane—she's obviously making good friends in Miami.

"It's so nice of you to travel all this way to be here for your friend," I say to Christine.

"We'll take any excuse to get out of Minnesota," she says, laughing loudly. "And I get to see my gorgeous baby girl which is always a bonus." She reaches over and pushes a strand of hair behind Sara's ear.

"Have you met my Sara's sweetheart, Dr. Calvin Sims?"

It's been years since I've heard someone refer to Cal by his full name.

"Yes, I've met Cal."

"Aren't they precious? I'm sure we'll be hearing wedding bells for the future Dr. and Mrs. Sims any day."

Thankfully, Diane arrives just in time to save the day. All attention shifts toward her as she squeals when she hugs each one of her guests.

"Lila. Having you here makes this day even more perfect. You're so thoughtful."

I give her a warm smile. "Well, when Sara invited me, I knew I couldn't miss it."

She claps her hands together. "I just love that you two have become friends. I knew you'd hit it off."

Sara nods. "And I have more exciting news—Cal and I are talking about buying Lila's home. It's a gorgeous house."

Cal was right, she doesn't let up.

"That's wonderful," Diane squeals. "Lila, when are you moving out?"

I give a noncommittal shrug. "I'm not sure. I've been living there with some friends the past few months. The house isn't up for sale yet."

I feel like I need to reiterate that fact over and over. Maybe at some point this girl will take the hint.

Unfortunately, it goes right over her head, and she continues talking about living next door to their close friends Theo and Gabby after they get married.

Maybe she's just not in touch with reality or she believes she'll be able to talk Cal into it eventually. Clearly she doesn't know that he and I talked about it.

"That would be so special," Diane says. "You two will be connected for life, and then you can go back and visit the house."

Nope. Just hearing her say that makes me cringe internally. It will be hard enough knowing that someone else is living in my childhood home. Sara and Cal there together feels wrong on so many levels. Ugh. I think I need a drink. I quickly excuse myself and make my way over to the bar. I usually don't day drink, but when in Rome ...

Sara invites everyone to sit down. "We're waiting on one more guest, but she should be here any minute."

While we wait, Diane begins talking about a few projects she's working on at the new house, and of course the attention shifts back to me. One of her friends, Carole, asks how long I've been doing real estate, and the conversation takes a turn. Sara picks up her phone and starts scrolling. I have a feeling she's growing tired of Diane's praise of me.

A few seconds later, Sara jumps to her feet to greet someone at the entrance. I feel like I've seen the woman before, and I watch curiously as she approaches the table. All of a sudden, my heart sinks.

Diane stands up to greet her. "Louise, thank you for coming."

It's Louise Sims, or as I know her, Mrs. Sims. Otherwise known as Cal's mom. She has a few more wrinkles around her eyes and the same wavy blonde hair.

This totally makes sense. Of course Diane knows Cal's mom. Sara and Cal have been together for a long time, and they've probably had a few happy family get-togethers by now. Christine is next to jump to her feet and give her a hug. All of a sudden I feel like the uninvited guest at a family reunion. I need to think, and quick. Pretending like I don't know her will make things even more awkward, and although Cal said she remembers me, I'm not convinced.

Diane begins making introductions, and when she comes to me, I give Cal's mom a warm smile.

"Hi, Mrs. Sims. You probably don't remember me."

A huge smile spreads across her face. "Oh my goodness, Lila Barlow. Of course I do."

She engulfs me in a hug that only a favorite teacher could give. She was never one my teachers, but she treated all the kids the same. She gives me one final squeeze before letting go.

"How do you know each other?" Diane asks.

"Cal and Lila went to high school together, remember," Sara answers for us. She shoots me a glance letting me know that she doesn't want anyone to know about my history with Cal.

Mrs. Sims gives a nod. "And I taught school for years and made it a point to know as many of the kids as I could."

I'm actually glad she redirected the conversation. This table of ladies doesn't need to know that Sara and I have similar interests other than fashion sense.

Our lunch continues, and we all share some of our favorite stories about Diane. She looks over the moon that everyone came to celebrate her, and I'm happy for her.

When a few of the ladies walk over to the bar, Mrs. Sims slides to the chair next to me.

"It's such a treat to see you," she says patting my hand. "Cal was just telling me about how you all reconnected."

I nod. "Yes, it's been very interesting."

"Tell me what you're up to."

What is there to say? I do real estate, but my agency is closing. I love living in my childhood home with the greatest roommates, but we're selling the house. I just broke up with a great guy. Ugh. Not a chance. Like my mom always says, fake it until your face hurts.

"My job keeps me extremely busy. And I love to travel when I can," I say with a shrug.

"How are your parents?"

"They're great. They are loving retirement and traveling."

"Retirement is wonderful. I golf and do Zumba now." She laughs while shaking her head. "If anyone would've told me years ago that those would be my hobbies, I would've said they were crazy."

"Cal told me that you still feed him and his friends once in a while."

She sighs. "Yes, much to my husband's dismay. But my boy needs to eat, and he works so hard taking care of other people."

I grin. "He was meant to be a doctor."

"That's what I always say."

Sara returns and sits down next to Mrs. Sims. "Isn't it fun, that we've all become friends?" she coos. "And this lady is one of the best."

She squeezes Mrs. Sims hand.

"And like Diane said, if you buy my house we'll be connected forever," I add.

Mrs. Sims smile fades, and she gives me a confused look.

"What house?"

Sara shoots me a dirty look.

Oops.

In my defense, we were just discussing this before Louise arrived. So how was I to know that we weren't supposed to talk about it in front of Cal's mom?

Sara quickly explains that they briefly discussed purchasing my parents' house. Of course it sounds different when she explains it to Louise. Hmm … I'm starting to wonder if Sara is just a big liar.

The party quickly shifts back to being about Diane and her opening the gifts. I think she might cry tears of joy when she opens my card and finds gift cards to HomeGoods. But who wouldn't? Everyone loves HomeGoods.

After the cake is served, I'm ready to make my exit. Although part of me wants to stay and talk to Mrs. Sims some more. She has the same warm and nurturing presence that I remember.

"I hope you had fun," Sara says before I leave.

"I did. Thank you so much for including me … I'm sorry if I said too much about the house in front of Cal's mom."

She waves her hand. "It's fine. I just think she'd rather us get married before moving in together."

My stomach twists into tiny knots at the thought.

"You never know. Look at Gabby and Theo."

She nods. "Yes, that happened very fast. But my grandmother used to say that nothing can stop love."

I purse my lips. I wish I believed that.

"That reminds me, were you able to get AJ's info for me? If not, it's fine. I'm sure I can get it from Theo."

She shakes her head. "Not yet, I've been so busy with this party. I'll try to talk to Cal about it."

Yes, please do that.

"Great. Maybe we can all go out for a drink or something," I say eagerly.

"Uh, sure. That sounds fun."

I pick up my Mountain Dew party favor and say my goodbyes, including one last big hug from Mrs. Sims.

Talk about an interesting day. I definitely didn't expect to see Cal's mom. And he was right, she does remember me.

I stretch out on the couch and pull a cozy blanket tightly around me. I've learned a lot today, including the fact that Mountain Dew isn't as bad as I thought. I couldn't drink it twenty-four hours a day like Diane does, but it's not terrible. I hear the door open, and Gabby walks into the kitchen.

"Hey," I say, holding up my bottle.

She gives me a funny look. "Are you drinking Mountain Dew?"

She sits on the edge of the couch while I tell her about Diane's birthday lunch and about seeing Cal's mom.

She laughs. "How did you get into this mess?"

I shake my head. "I've been wondering the same thing all day."

We're still chatting when Reagan comes in.

"Hey, Reagan," Gabby calls.

"Hey."

She walks into the living room and puts her hands on her hips. It doesn't take a genius to know that something's wrong.

"Lila, is it true?" she asks sharply. "We have to move out?"

A lump quickly forms in the back of my throat. Gabby furrows her brow and gives me a concerned look. "What's going on?"

I let out a sigh.

So many thoughts are flying around in my head, and the truth is that I don't have a good reason for waiting to tell them.

"My parents want to the sell the house," I say. "Not immediately."

"But sometime soon, right?" Reagan asks. "Why would you keep that from us?"

"I wasn't keeping it from you," I trail off. "I was going to wait until after Theo's party, and then the engagement happened. I just didn't know how to break the bad news."

Reagan folds her arms. "Seriously? You don't think that we can handle bad news? I think we deserve to know if we're going to be homeless or not."

I lean my head to the side. "That's being a bit dramatic, don't you think?"

Gabby still hasn't said anything. Of course, she's engaged, and she could move in with Theo at any moment.

"No. I don't think I'm being dramatic. I think you should've told us the night you found out. And now I look stupid in front of Bethany because I defended you. I told her that you would never keep something like that from me."

Hold on. What is she talking about?

"Bethany? That's how you found out?"

She nods. "Yep. Of all people."

I'm so confused. Did Paul tell her? He's definitely on the top of my list now.

"You told Bethany before us," Gabby exclaims.

"Of course not."

"Then how did she find out?"

I'm trying to think of all the people that I know. Ugh. There are a lot. I guess I have some explaining to do.

"I told Paul and Harry when we were on the boat. Either Paul told her, or she overheard me. I'm not sure."

Reagan frowns.

"So you decided to talk to them about it while you were sipping a cocktail without a care in the world."

I've only seen Reagan mad a few times and only when Bethany was involved. I'm not surprised Bethany used this to her advantage—well played.

"Are you kidding?" I shout. "I've been struggling with it since I found out. Not only do we all have to leave, but I have to say good-bye to my childhood home. And to make things worse, Sara thinks that she and Cal should buy it."

Reagan and Gabby exchange a glance.

"Yes, Sara and Cal know," I mutter. "But only because they showed up to the restaurant when I was having dinner with my parents. The Hillards had to sit near us, and they heard our conversation."

Neither of my roommates say anything for a few seconds.

"I understand why you didn't say anything before the party, but you've had plenty of time since then," Reagan says finally. "And to have to hear it from Bethany is the worst-case scenario."

"I know, and believe me, I never wanted it to come from her."

"Who else knows?" Gabby asks.

I chew on my lip. I don't want to tell her that Theo knows, but I don't want to keep anything from her.

"Well, Sara brought it up at Diane's birthday lunch. So, all of her friends know," I say with a shrug.

"Does Theo know?" Gabby asks.

Crap.

"Yes, but I didn't tell him. That was Cal."

She shakes her head.

"Please don't be mad at him," I beg. "He just found out before he left on the trip, and I asked him not to say anything because I wanted to be the one to talk to you guys about it. Obviously Bethany ruined that like she does everything else."

There's an uncomfortable tension in the room. I shouldn't have let it go this long. I'm not even sure why I waited anymore.

"Look, I'm really sorry. I guess it was just too hard to face the fact that everything in my life is changing. If I didn't tell you, then I could avoid the inevitable."

Reagan sits down on the couch, her face softening slightly.

"So, when are you putting the house on the market?" Gabby asks.

I sigh. "My parents said we didn't have to do it right away, but I know they're anxious to get it done. I have to touch base with them once I have a timeframe that works for all of us. They would never force me to do it if we don't have somewhere else to live."

I can feel tears threatening my eyes, but I hold them in. I need to hold it together—it's not like I haven't left home before.

"I'm guessing Bethany reached out to you despite my trying to discourage her."

Reagan nodded. "She texted me a few days ago, but I ignored it and deleted the message. Today she called me from a number I didn't recognize. I fell right into her trap."

"And she used me to help her case."

She nods. "She told me that she had some important news that you were keeping from me and Gabby."

For once Bethany wasn't lying.

"Why does everything have to happen all at once?" Gabby asks. "Fun in the Sun is closing, and now we have to find a new place to live."

Reagan looks stunned. "What?"

Gabby tells her about Elizabeth's London plans.

"Wow, I'm sorry to hear that."

Speaking of keeping things from people, I haven't even told Gabby that Elizabeth asked if I'd take over the agency. I'm definitely not saying anything tonight. There's been enough news for one day.

"You both have every right to be upset with me," I say glumly. "I just hope that we're able to make the most of the time we have left together in this house."

Reagan's eyes fill with tears, prompting Gabby to move next to her and put her arm around her.

I try to force the lump in my throat away, but it doesn't disappear. My roommates both start crying, and before I know it, I give up the fight. A single tear slides down my cheek, and I quickly wipe it away.

Once again I'm reminded that life keeps moving fast no matter how hard we try to slow it down.

Chapter Fourteen

I feel sick to my stomach. It could be the pizza, the stress, or maybe the Mountain Dew. Does anyone really know what's in that drink?

After my roommates and I had a good cry, we ordered food and talked about what lies ahead for us.

I know Reagan is still upset with me, and I feel bad about it. My intentions were good. It just sucks that Bethany of all people had to be the one to break the bad news to her. And I know she's going to use that to her advantage and try to slither her way back into Reagan's life.

"So, Sara told you that she and Cal want to buy the house?" Gabby asked. "That's awkward."

"I know. The interesting thing is that Cal told me that it's not true. He even went out of his way to text me after Theo talked to him."

Thankfully, Gabby isn't mad at Theo for not telling her. The last thing I want is to cause problems for the newly engaged couple.

"So he doesn't want to move in with her?" Gabby asks.

I shake my head. "No, he does—I think. He just said they wouldn't be buying this house because there are too many memories."

Gabby raises her eyebrows. "Of you?"

I start to pull on a loose string from the throw pillow in my lap. "He didn't say."

"But that's what he meant," she says knowingly.

I shrug. "Does it really matter?"

"Yes. Because I think there's a part of Cal that might still have a feeling or two for you."

"A feeling or two?" I repeat.

"Yep, and I think it's mutual."

I could sit here and insist that I haven't felt anything since Cal fell back into my life, but they know better. "So what if I do? He's with Sara."

"Until AJ Bennett comes around," Gabby suggests.

Ugh. I don't know what to think anymore.

"We should have a dinner party," Reagan announces, like it's the most brilliant idea she's ever come up with.

Gabby and I both give her a curious look.

"I hope you're not suggesting we make dinner and invite guests over to eat it," I ask.

She snorts. "Definitely not. But, since our days are numbered here, we could do a potluck. Everyone could bring a dish, and you could invite AJ. Then we could all witness how Sara acts around him. If there's something going on, Cal deserves to know."

The corner of Gabby's mouth curls up. "A dinner party. It could be fun—and you're right, it may be one of our last here."

Reagan shrugs. "And if there's really nothing going on with Sara and AJ, then Lila can make her move on him. He's super handsome and seems like he'd be a lot of fun."

Reagan smiles proudly at her sneaky idea.

Well, well, well, I knew there was a devious side to Reagan under all the kindness and understanding. I'm grateful she's still talking to me after I withheld important information.

This ought to be interesting. Let the games begin.

～

"Hi, honey. How are sales?" my mother asks.

I groan as I finish typing an email. I have so much on my plate right now that sales are the last thing on my mind.

"I have a condo closing at the end of the week."

"Excellent."

"Speaking of sales, I have some news," I say. I'm just about to tell my mother about Fun in the Sun, but she starts talking before I have a chance.

"Great, I was hoping you were ready to move forward with listing the house."

I let out a frustrated sigh. "Um, not yet—but soon."

I explain that Elizabeth is moving to London and will probably close the agency. I'm hoping this will convince her to delay the house a least until Gabby and I figure out where we want to land.

"Oh no, I'm sorry to hear that."

"Me too. It's been a rough few weeks."

My mother and I don't have the type of relationship for me to cry on her shoulder. She means well, but she's not a Mrs. Sims type. I remember coming home from school upset about friends or boys and she would tell me that my heartache would help me in the future and make me a stronger person. It was always good advice, but sometimes I just wanted her to give me a bowl of ice cream and a hug.

"I'm sure there will be companies fighting to add you to their teams."

I was going to tell her about Elizabeth's offer, but I hold

back. I haven't shared this with anyone yet, and the last thing I need is added pressure from my mother.

"Have you spoken to your roommates yet?" she asks.

"Yes, they're both really sad."

"I'm sure. Maybe you could all find a lovely house to rent."

"Yeah, we haven't had a chance to discuss it," I say. "You told me I had time."

"You do. I just don't want you to wait too long."

"I'm not. I have the landscaper coming on Friday. And I'm going to do a walk-through checklist this weekend."

"Wonderful," she says excitedly. "Have you seen Cal Sims recently?"

I almost fall off my chair. What on earth would make her ask about Cal?

"No, why?"

"I was just curious."

"Mom?"

She sighs into the phone. "Okay. I've been thinking about how we ran into him at the restaurant. Daddy said he kept looking over at you throughout the evening."

Huh. My parents have never gotten involved in my personal life. They've met a few of the men I've dated from time to time, but they always cared more about my success than my relationships.

"Cal's girlfriend wants them to buy the house," I blurt out.

As soon as I say the words out loud, I regret it. She's probably going to tell me to close the deal ASAP.

"They can't buy our house," she shouts.

Whoa. I didn't expect that reaction.

"They aren't. Cal said no when she suggested it."

"I should think so."

I breathe a sigh of relief that my big mouth didn't get me in trouble.

"Anyway, I'll keep you updated on everything. Where are you off to next?"

I know that the best way to shift my mother's focus is to talk about their next trip. I listen as she goes on and on about their upcoming visit to the Oregon coast.

Just as I'm ending the call, Gabby turns around in her chair, with a mischievous smile on her face. We are the only two in the office right now.

"Guess who's coming to dinner."

I raise my eyebrows.

"Theo talked to AJ and told him we were having a casual dinner party, and he's in."

Theo is really stepping up his game lately. I almost feel bad about all the terrible things I've said about him over the years—almost.

"Apparently, he was really interested in learning more about you."

I chew on my pen cap.

"Do you think we're wrong about him and Sara?" I ask. "I mean if they were doing anything, would he be asking questions about me?"

"I was thinking about that."

All of a sudden I wonder if this poor guy is innocent. What if he's just getting a bad rap because he's a big flirt?

"I guess we'll find out," she says with a shrug.

Gabby returns to her desk, and I scroll through my client list.

I have one closing this week, and I'm waiting on two other offers. Elizabeth hasn't approached me about taking over the agency, and I've been avoiding it.

Is all this avoidance a coping mechanism? I avoided telling my roommates about the house, and that made it worse. This reminds me that I have to call Paul and ask him why he told Bethany about the house. He knows better than to discuss my life with her.

I scroll through my phone and find his number. I send him a quick text.

Call me.

Not even two minutes goes by when my phone rings.

"You summoned me?"

"Very funny," I say. "I'm surprised you actually called me back so fast."

"I figured I might as well take my beating and get it over with."

Paul has an amazing way of twisting things so it's hard to stay mad at him.

"How could you?" I shout. "I told you Bethany was trouble."

"I know, I know."

"Wait. So you're actually admitting it? Hang on, I need a witness." I put my speaker phone on so Gabby can listen.

"Gabby's here too. Why would you tell her about the house? She called Reagan and tried to wreak havoc like usual."

He's quiet for a few seconds. "Lila, what are you talking about?"

I look at Gabby and roll my eyes.

"What do you think? Bethany. You just agreed that she was trouble."

"Yeah, but I didn't tell her about the house. I was talking about her and Jordan."

Jordan? My Jordan, or my ex-Jordan.

Gabby's mouth drops open.

"Are you saying that Bethany and Jordan are seeing each other?" I exclaim.

Paul is silent. Obviously he thought that's why I wanted to talk to him.

"I don't know the specifics," he says finally. "I just know that that they've been out a few times since seeing each other on the boat."

Like I said, I didn't expect it to be long before some lucky woman snagged Jordan. I just never in a million years thought that woman would be Bethany.

"Anyway, you were right. Harry was right. I was wrong."

At least he's finally seeing Bethany's true colors. I do feel bad for him though. Paul never seems to be lucky when it comes to love, but part of that is because he always goes for the wrong women. Women like Bethany who see the family money and overlook the fun-loving good guy that he is.

"Maybe Jordan told her about the house?" Paul suggests.

"I don't think he knows about it. We had already broken up before I had dinner with my parents ... Oh well, it doesn't matter anyway."

I'm still trying to wrap my head around the fact that Jordan is seeing that evil woman. We were together when she was staying here. I even vented to him about her a few times.

"Are you okay?" he asks.

"Obviously I'm not thrilled," I say. "I'm afraid Jordan will have to learn the hard way like you and Reagan did."

Paul gets another call, so our conversation is cut short.

"Maybe Bethany and Jordan are just friends," Gabby suggests. "It wouldn't be the first time she tried to get her claws into a great guy."

"You're right," I say thoughtfully. "Either way, it's no longer my business. I care about Jordan, but I knew we were over long before I ended things."

Chapter Fifteen

My skills in the kitchen are mostly pathetic, but I can make an Instagram-worthy charcuterie board. My roommates and are I prepping for the dinner party we're hosting for Theo, Cal, Sara, AJ, and Reagan's boyfriend, Jeremy. I put on some background music, and we're singing along to the best music hits of the 90s. There are a few moments when I feel that familiar lump forming in my throat. Every time I think about not having more evenings like this, I want to cry. Ugh, Lila Barlow doesn't cry—she fakes it until her face hurts.

The impending move is kind of like the elephant in the room at this point. We all know it needs to be addressed, but none of us want to actually bring it up. I've already started looking at some properties, and there are plenty of great homes out there. Unfortunately, none of them compare to this house.

"This smells divine," Reagan says, lifting the cover off the chicken masala we ordered. She's wearing a blue halter dress with a cream-colored sweater over it. Her blonde hair is full of bouncy waves.

Gabby's busy trying to open a bottle of wine. She's wearing a pair of dark skinny jeans with an oversized black sweater. Her brown hair is pulled into a high ponytail on top of her head.

I decided on a black flowy maxi dress and wrapped a scarf around my hair like a headband.

There's a knock on the door, and Reagan hurries to answer it.

"Hey, blondie," a deep voice says. Reagan returns to the kitchen holding a large box from Donut Giant. Her boyfriend Jeremy has a severe addiction to the donut shop that makes the best donuts ever, although you'd never know it by looking at him. He's that guy that can eat three donuts and then run ten miles to work them off. Yes, it's super annoying. Reagan's sister nicknamed him Mr. Abs.

"Hello, ladies. Thanks for inviting me to dinner. You can put me to work—serving, cleaning, spying … I'm your guy."

Reagan hits him on the arm.

"Oh sorry, is someone else here?" he whispers.

"No, you're fine," I tell him. "Thanks for the donuts."

The doorbell rings again.

"Show time," Jeremy exclaims.

Gabby giggles, while Reagan smacks him on the arm again.

This time I head to answer the door. When I open it, I find Sara and Cal waiting there. Sara forces a smile, but it's very obvious that she's bothered by something.

"Hey, girl. You won't believe it, but I almost wore a similar dress."

I laugh. "I believe it. Come in."

She walks in and looks around the house. "I still feel like this could be our house," she exclaims as she heads toward the kitchen.

Cal lets out an exasperated sigh and hands me a serving dish. "This is from my mom—her homemade potato casserole and her orange crescent rolls are in this bag."

"Awe—that was so thoughtful of her."

"Sara asked her to make something because she doesn't like to cook."

Figures. "I know the feeling."

Our hands touch when I take the dish from him, which causes a jolt of something electric to shoot through my body.

"Is everything okay?" I ask, pointing toward the kitchen.

"Yes, she's just mad at me again."

Again?

There's another knock on the door. Cal opens it since my hands are full.

"Hey, hey, Dr. Sims," AJ booms.

He's holding a gorgeous bouquet of flowers.

"Evening, Dr. Bennett," Cal says firmly.

They both start laughing.

AJ gives me a smoldering smile and leans in to kiss me on the cheek. "Hello, beautiful."

Good hell, this man is smooth.

When I glance at Cal, he's noticeably irritated.

"Come on in, guys," I announce.

When we enter the kitchen, I see that Theo has also arrived. Of course, he just uses the back door now. That's the beauty of being able to come through the backyard.

The next few minutes are full of introductions and serving drinks. AJ makes himself right at home, pouring glasses of wine for everyone and chatting up Jeremy. I can see why everyone says he's the life of the party. Like clockwork, Sara inserts herself into AJ and Jeremy's conversation.

Gabby, Reagan, and I all exchange a glance. My charcuterie board is a hit, and a discussion breaks out about the name while Jeremy insists that it should just be called a snack platter. Everything is going very smoothly, although I can't help but notice that Cal is definitely more quiet than usual.

"Cal, are these your mom's orange rolls?" AJ exclaims. "I still dream about these things. She used to send them when we'd work those long hospital shifts."

"Yes, Mom's rolls are famous," he agrees.

I overhear Gabby talking to Sara about the similarities of Theo's house and ours. I guess she hasn't given up yet. Maybe that's why she's mad at Cal *again*. Reagan, Jeremy, and Cal walk out onto the patio, leaving AJ and me sitting together at the kitchen counter.

"Thanks for inviting me tonight. I don't get many dinner invitations," he says, the corner of his mouth tilting up.

He can't be serious. I'm not sure who he thinks he's talking to but, there's no way I'm falling for that.

"Oh, sure you do," I reply.

"Actually, I don't. I work a lot, but I'm trying to cut back to allow more time for my hobbies," he says running his hand through his hair, making it fall perfectly to cup his chiseled face.

"Wait, are you saying that you don't just have fun while making your brother do all the other stuff?"

He chuckles. "I forgot I told you about that."

I lean against the counter. "You did, and I don't forget things."

AJ moves closer to me. "I'm fascinated by you, Lila."

Before I can respond, Sara joins us.

"Lila, thanks again for coming to celebrate Diane's birthday. She was so happy you were there."

"You're very welcome," I say. "It was so lovely. You did a great job."

She puts her elbows on the counter and casually leans over right in front of AJ.

Damn, I wish I could figure this girl out. One minute she's talking about a magical future with Cal, and the next she's trying to get AJ to notice her. Maybe it's all about the attention, or the fact that AJ exudes mystery. Cal is definitely handsome, but AJ gives off the textbook bad boy vibe. There's obviously a part of Sara that's attracted to that.

"AJ was just telling me that he rarely gets dinner invitations," I tell her.

She pretends to look shocked. "Oh, no. That's a shame."

He pouts. "It is a shame. Hopefully that changes and Lila will invite me over again."

Sara plasters a fake smile on her face. "I'm sure she will once she gets settled in a new place, right, Lila? This gorgeous house is about to be sold."

I nod sadly.

"Really? This is a great house. I'd love a tour sometime later," he says.

"Yes, me too," Sara chimes in.

The conversation shifts to real estate, and Sara continues her subtle flirtation. I don't pick up on anything unusual from either of them, which makes me wonder if I was wrong. Maybe there isn't anything going on other than the casual flirting. I excuse myself to talk to my roommates, leaving them alone in the kitchen. Reagan, Gabby, Theo, Jeremy, and Cal are out on the patio talking about the hammock incident. Gabby catches my eye and walks over to me.

"What's up?"

I shake my head. "Nothing."

She leans her head to the side. "I don't believe you."

I glance over to see Cal watching us, and I instantly feel like a terrible person for thinking his girlfriend was cheating on him. The last thing I'd ever want is for him to be hurt. He's been with Sara for three years—he obviously loves her.

"I'm good. Let's get ready for dinner."

Gabby and I go back inside the house, and Sara and AJ are no longer in the kitchen.

She looks at me, her eyes growing wide.

"Where did they go?" she mouths.

I shrug my shoulders.

Gabby looks outside and shakes her head.

My heart starts to pound inside my chest.

They could be anywhere, but I'm trying not to jump to any more conclusions. It wouldn't shock me if they're just wandering around, taking their own tour of the house since Sara is still determined to move in here. And would they actually do something with all of us here? Suddenly I'm reminded that Theo said he wouldn't trust AJ around his girlfriend. A knot is rapidly forming in the pit of my stomach.

Most of the living space including the kitchen is in the middle of the house. The bedrooms are all nestled in opposite corners with their own bathrooms. The floor plan is brilliant, and a seller's dream come true.

I'm just about to go look for them when Cal walks into the kitchen. "Do you two need any help?"

Holy crap, this is awkward.

"I think we're good," Gabby says, holding up both her thumbs. I know she's trying to diffuse the situation. "Everything is almost ready."

"We just need to round everyone up in a few minutes," I tell him. For some reason I can't take my eyes off him. Cal Sims is back in my kitchen after all these years, and we're no longer teenagers. This is real life—and real life is messy.

"Where's Sara?" I ask.

Cal furrows his eyebrows, and I almost see the wheels turning in his head.

Without a word, he takes off to find her. Gabby gives me a look, and I grit my teeth. What type of people have the nerve to sneak off and hook up at a dinner party—with Cal here? Not even two seconds later, AJ and Sara return to the kitchen.

"I might have to consider buying this house," AJ exclaims.

"We just took a little tour," Sara adds. "But I told him I have first dibs."

Sara's face is flushed, but AJ seems as relaxed as ever. Is it possible they were just checking out the house? Sure. Do I believe that was it? Nope.

I few seconds later, Cal returns. He's visibly upset, but he doesn't say anything. The rest of the guests join us in the kitchen, completely oblivious that anything is off.

"Help yourself," I announce. "We'll be eating in my mother's formal dining room which I think has been used ten times in my entire life."

Didn't everyone have one of these rooms in their childhood home? Our guests continue chatting as they dig in. Cal hangs back, sipping his wine, a vacant look in his eyes. There's a part of me that wants to rush to be by his side, but I wait.

After everyone else heads to the dining room, I pick up a plate and hand it to him.

"Are you hungry?"

He shakes his head.

"Not even for one of your mother's famous orange rolls?" I ask, trying to lighten the mood. "I've already had three, but don't tell anyone."

He musters up a faint smile.

I wish there was something I could say, but there's nothing. I certainly don't know if something just happened with Sara and AJ, but I have a feeling Cal does. I can't imagine how he's feeling. Theo said he and Sara were having issues, and in the back of my mind I keep wondering if there's a reason he hasn't proposed to her yet.

"You should get back to your guests," he says softly. "I'll be there in a minute."

"Okay." I hesitate. I put some food on my plate and head to my mother's barely used dining room. Gabby and Reagan both give me curious looks as soon as I walk in.

"How is everything?" I ask as I sit down.

"Where's Cal?" Sara asks, holding up her wine glass.

Why do you care?

"He said he'd be in here in a minute."

All of a sudden the front door slams. Sara turns white as a ghost.

"Excuse me. I'll be right back." She hurries out of the dining room, and I glance at AJ who's munching on one of Mrs. Sims's orange rolls. All of sudden he's not as attractive as I thought he was.

Jeremy steps up and saves the day with a story, but I'm barely listening to him. I can't stop thinking about Cal. For years I was angry at him for breaking my heart. He was my first love, and do you ever completely get over your first love? I believe there's a place in your heart that they always hold, no matter what your life brings.

I'm not sure what he's thinking right now or what's really going on, but I have a feeling this thing with AJ and Sara isn't new. I saw their interaction at Theo's birthday party, and although it's hard to imagine that people could do such a thing—it happens. I've learned that life isn't a fairy tale, but I still have hope that true happiness exists. No matter what, I still believe in the one person who our souls are meant to find. My grandma used to say that you have to kiss a lot of frogs to find your prince.

The door slams again. I'm guessing that Sara went after Cal and, judging by the loss of color in her face, she's panicking.

Chapter Sixteen

My mother always loved to entertain, partly to show off her latest house project. Anyway, we always had people over—holiday parties, women's clubs, pool parties. I enjoyed it because otherwise the house was really quiet.

Sara and Cal don't return before we finish eating.

Our dinner party continues, and AJ makes every attempt to ask me questions like we're on our first date. I play my part and answer them while my mind is far away, wondering if Cal is okay.

Reagan, Gabby, and I meet up in the kitchen while the men continue chatting at the table.

"I'm totally confused," Reagan whispers. "What's going on?"

Gabby turns on water in the sink and explains what we assume happened. Reagan's mouth drops open.

"Did he catch them together?" she asks.

"I don't think so, but he was pissed."

"AJ seems fine," Reagan says.

I frown. "Don't get me started on him. I don't understand any of this. Isn't he supposed to be their friend?"

Theo joins us in the kitchen. "Where's Cal?"

"I don't know, but I'm worried. Will you call him and make sure he's okay?" I beg.

He takes his phone out of his pocket. "I'm on it."

Theo walks outside, and I watch out the window as he starts walking back and forth. I can tell that he's talking to him. A few seconds later he comes back inside.

"Is he okay?"

"Yes. He apologized for leaving."

"Is Sara with him?" Gabby asks.

He nods. "Yes. He said they were having a long overdue conversation and got off the phone very quickly."

I'd give anything to listen in on that conversation.

"Is anyone else ready for donuts?" Jeremy asks, coming into the kitchen.

"I am. There's always room for donuts," AJ chimes in from right behind him.

Reagan grabs some plates and takes the box out to the patio. I mindlessly load the dishwasher while thinking about all the possible scenarios of Cal and Sara's conversation. Cal was preoccupied when they arrived, so maybe there's more going on than we know. Regardless, I haven't heard AJ say one word about either of them being gone.

AJ and I are the last two in the kitchen, so I take advantage of the moment.

"I hope everything is okay with Cal and Sara. They left so abruptly."

He shrugs. "I'm sure they're fine."

Unbelievable.

"Is there anything else I can get for you?" I ask coldly.

"Besides a date with you?"

Not a chance.

"I'm flattered, but I'm not sure we're compatible," I say with a shrug.

He runs his hand through his hair. I have a feeling that's one of his trademark moves that make the women fall at his feet. "How do you know?"

"Just a feeling."

He slides closer to me. "You won't know until you give it a try."

"I don't think so, but thanks for coming tonight," I say sweetly. "I hope you had a nice evening."

I walk outside to join my friends, leaving AJ to question himself why a woman turned him down and the meaning of life.

It doesn't take long after my rejection for AJ to take the hint. He says his good-byes and leaves abruptly. Once he's gone, we're free to talk about what went down during the dinner party from hell. We all share our own observations, but I think Jeremy has the most likely scenario.

"That was all her," he says. "AJ couldn't care less, but I'm sure if she put it out there, he wasn't going to turn it down."

"I don't understand. How could he do that to Cal?" Reagan wonders aloud.

Theo sighs. "AJ doesn't think. He lives in the moment."

"That's terrible," Reagan adds.

"I agree," Theo says.

"He asked me out, and I turned him down flat."

"Good," Theo says. "That's probably why he left so quickly."

We talk for a while. Jeremy finally leaves a little after midnight, and Gabby walks Theo home.

"You okay?" Reagan asks.

"Yeah, just tired."

"That was an eventful dinner party," she says.

I laugh. "It was your idea."

"Yeah, next time I have an idea like that, you should remind me of this."

We say good night, and I head to my bathroom to get ready for bed. As I wash my face, I keep checking my phone with the hopes that Cal might text me. I'm sure sending me a message is the last thing on his mind tonight. I just want to know that he's all right, and there's a part of me that's feeling guilty for hosting the nightmare get-together. I finally crawl into bed and stare up at the ceiling.

I have a lot of other things to think about that have nothing to do with Cal Sims's personal life. I'm done living in the past, and its time move on, starting with this house. Tomorrow I will officially begin the search for my new home. It's time.

I'm about to doze off when there's a knock on my door. Gabby sticks her head in my room.

"Hey, are you still awake?"

"Barely."

"Cal's here."

I shoot out of bed like a cannon. "What?"

"He called Theo while I was there, and we invited him to come over. I can tell him you're already in bed."

"No, it's okay."

It doesn't matter that I have no makeup on or that I'm wearing a faded pair of flannel pajamas.

I follow Gabby out to the living room. Cal is sitting on the edge of the couch staring down at his phone.

"Hey."

He looks up from his phone.

"I'm headed to bed," Gabby says. "Good night."

"We're you asleep?" he asks.

I sit down next to him and curl one leg under me.

"Not yet … Are you hungry?"

He nods. "I'm starving."

"We have tons of food left, including plenty of orange rolls that I confiscated. Come on."

Cal doesn't argue, and we make our way to the kitchen. I start taking food out of the fridge and hand him a bottle of water.

"Thank you, Lila."

I smile. "Sure."

I ask him what he wants and start preparing a plate for him.

"This about the extent of my kitchen skills," I joke. "Heating up food that I didn't prepare."

He puts his elbows on the counter and leans his chin on his hands.

"I'm sorry that I made a scene at your dinner. I'm so embarrassed."

I wait for the microwave to count down and take the plate out.

"You have nothing to apologize for."

I'm dying to know what happened with him and Sara, but I'm not going to ask. I'll let him share what he wants to.

"Your mom hasn't lost her touch. Everything was delicious."

He nods. "She's the best. I almost went over there tonight, but I didn't want to have to answer a bunch of questions."

And that's exactly why I'm not going to ask him anything.

"I was shocked that she actually remembered me," I admit.

"I told you."

"You did, but she's met hundreds of kids."

"She remembers her favorites," he says, before taking a bite of chicken.

"I never had her as a teacher," I say, leaning against the counter. "My friend Shelley was in her class, and she used to brag that your mom would bring Fun-Dips on Fridays."

He laughs. "Oh yeah, those packets of sugar were damn good."

We both grow quiet.

"Speaking of sugar. Jeremy left a bunch of donuts."

I grab the box and sit down next to him. The sugary devils smell intoxicating. Too bad I already brushed my teeth.

"Sara and I broke up," he blurts out.

Well, I guess he's ready to talk about it after all. Now what am I supposed to say? I'm sorry? Good for you? About time?

"You don't have to talk about it, if you don't want to."

"It's fine," he says. "I'm sure you'll hear from her or Diane, so I might as well give you my side first."

"Okay."

"It was only a matter of time. We've been trying to make it work for a while now, even though we'd been growing apart. After three years, it's hard to just give up."

I listen intently. I want to ask all the questions. Instead I let him get it all out of his system.

"She's had a thing for AJ for a while—I knew but I just ignored it, I guess. She's going to be very disappointed when she realizes that AJ isn't going to settle down anytime soon."

"He asked me out tonight," I tell him. "And I turned him down, which was really fun."

He pounds his hand on the counter. "Damn, I wish I could've seen that. Only AJ would ask someone out an hour after making out with someone else."

"Oh, so they?"

He nods. "Oh, yeah."

I knew it. None of this is shocking to me. I'm just amazed at how calm Cal is right now.

"Anyway, we had a long talk," he continues. "It got pretty ugly. She blames me because I wouldn't take the next step like buying this house."

"She really wanted this house, huh?"

He nods. "Of course."

I sigh. "I'm really sorry. You tried to warn me about AJ. Maybe if we hadn't had this dinner party none of this would've happened."

"It's definitely not your fault," he says. "We were fighting before we came here tonight and have been for months."

"You seem so calm."

He smiles. "That's the doctor in me. I'm an expert at keeping my cool in stressful situations."

"Interesting. I didn't think about that."

He pushes his nearly empty plate away and reaches for the donut box, brushing my arm with his. My pulse speeds up slightly and I quickly stand up to take his plate to the sink.

Thoughts about him and me are already swirling around in my head, and I need to push them out. He hasn't even been single for an hour yet.

"Can I get you some more water or something else to drink?"

"No, but I appreciate it," he says. "I should probably get out of your house though, it's the middle of the night."

"It's totally fine," I say, yawning. *Typical.*

Of course it is because I don't actually want him to leave.

He stands up.

"I have your mom's bowl. Do you want to take the rest of the rolls with you?"

He shakes his head. "Nope. Those are for you."

"Please thank her for me."

He starts to walk toward the front door, and I'm right behind him.

"Thanks for the food and for listening."

"Sure, I'm here anytime you want to talk."

He opens the door and gives me a wave. "Good night, Lila."

"Cal," I say with a nod.

He laughs.

I start to close the door, but before I do, he pushes it open and pulls me into his arms. He tightens his arms around me, and I melt into them. I must need this hug as much as he does because I hold on tight.

His body is warm and familiar, even after all the years that have passed. My head rests against his chest, and I feel his chin rest on the top of my head. His chest rises and falls against mine, and just as our hearts begin to beat at the same speed, he starts to pull away.

"Okay, I'm really leaving now."

No.

I watch as he walks into the darkness. After I close the door, my heart is still racing.

This night definitely took a turn I wasn't expecting, and I'm not complaining.

Chapter Seventeen

As soon as I open my eyes, the memories of last night flood my brain. Starting with the dinner party that went rogue and the surprise ending to the evening. The truth is that I'm not sad about Cal and Sara breaking up. Does this make me a terrible person? I know there are always two sides to every story and then there's the truth. I'm not expecting to hear from Sara, at least not today, considering the connection I have to Cal. I've only known her for a minute compared to him, so it wouldn't be unusual for me to take his side. The only complication is Diane Hillard. I have no doubt that she'll be Team Sara, and she doesn't know about my history with Cal. She's probably going to be devastated when she hears that Sara lost her lobster. Thank goodness we finished the deal before all of this went down, and this serves as a good lesson for me. I know better than to mix business and friendship. Of course clients can be friends, with appropriate boundaries.

I lie in bed for a while, which I rarely do, but it's Sunday. My parents used to say that doing this was time wasted, the early bird gets the worm and all that jazz. I have some big decisions to make that I've been avoiding.

Elizabeth hasn't brought up her offer, but I know she'll want an answer soon. I'm flattered, but I don't think I'm ready to give up the freedom I have. As much as I'd love to be the one to keep Fun in the Sun up and running, I don't think that role is for me. Right now I'm able to devote my time and energy to my clients, and that's one of the aspects that has brought me to this point in my career. The Hillards are a perfect example, before the Sara and Cal debacle.

I finally hop out of bed and head to the bathroom to get my day started. I've been mentally preparing myself to focus on finding my new home. The benefit of my job is that I always have my eyes open for amazing properties, and I'm sure I'll be able to find a great place to live. I loved my condo—it was in a great area near the beach, shopping, and some fabulous restaurants. I'm going to search the same area. I also need to have a conversation with my roommates. We're still avoiding the moving conversation, but it's time. I'd love to continue living with them if they're interested. Of course, Gabby and Theo may have had a different conversation now that they're engaged.

After dragging myself out of bed, I curl up with my coffee and my laptop on one of chaise lounges next to the pool. I've already answered five emails, and I'm working on a listing for a referral one of my clients sent over.

As hard as I try to focus on work, I keep thinking about Cal. I know how it feels to wake up the next morning after a breakup. Every aspect of your life is in flux, and even when you know it's the right decision, it's hard. Cal was with Sara for three years, so they must've cared deeply for each other. I don't know the intricate details of their relationship or what went wrong. I'm sure they hurt each other along the way. It happens even when it's not intended.

"Morning," Gabby says. She's wearing a *Miami* T-shirt that looks about two sizes too big, so I'm assuming it's Theo's. Her hair is all over the place, and she's wearing her glasses.

She plops down on the chair next to me and stretches her arms over her head.

"Tell me everything."

"What are you talking about?"

She rolls her eyes. "What do you think I'm talking about? When I went to bed, Cal was here."

I give a nonchalant shrug.

"Come on, Lila."

I laugh. "It was fine. I fed him, we talked, and he told me that he and Sara broke up."

Her eyes grow wide. "Wow. How was he taking it? He seemed fine when he got to Theo's. If anything, he was more concerned about running out on dinner."

I nod. "He was embarrassed about that."

She chews on her bottom lip. "I think this was a long time coming. When Theo and I first got together, he would tell me how happy Cal and Sara were together. But something always seemed off to me."

"Cal said they had been growing apart for some time. I think the AJ thing was the final nail in the coffin."

"So they did—"

"He didn't give me details, and I didn't want to ask. I tried really hard to just listen and not ask too many questions."

She nods. "That was good."

We're both quiet for a few seconds.

"Anyway, so that's it. I hope he's doing okay today. Maybe Theo can check on him?"

The corner of her mouth turns up. "Or you could."

"Yeah, but I'm not going to."

"Why?"

I don't have an answer for that.

"I'm sure he's dealing with a lot today," I say, pulling my knees into my chest.

"Which is why you should reach out to him."

"Maybe later."

While Gabby goes inside to make herself a cup of coffee, I think about what she said. Cal and I are friends, so why shouldn't I check in on him? He's the one who came here last night.

I'm about to reach for my phone when it rings. My heart does a flip. Maybe Cal will reach out to me first.

Except it's not him—it's Diane Hillard. Crap. That didn't take long. I consider letting it go to voice mail, but she'll continue calling until she gets me on the phone.

I take a deep breath and answer.

"Hello," I say cheerfully.

"Oh, Lila, I'm so glad you answered. Can you talk?" she asks, her voice in a panic. I guess this means she's heard the news of her precious Sara's breakup, or she's run out of Mountain Dew.

"Um, sure. Are you okay?"

I'm certainly not going to tell her that I talked to Cal just a few hours ago.

"David is giving me a hard time about calling you, but I knew you wouldn't care."

David Hillard is such a smart guy.

"First of all, I heard that something awful happened at your home last night. I'm so disappointed in Calvin's behavior, and I want to apologize for that."

Calvin's behavior?

Clearly Sara gave her the watered-down version of the story, conveniently leaving out the part about making out with Dr. AJ while her boyfriend and his friends were in the next room.

"He hasn't been himself lately, and last night was the last straw. He broke my Sara's heart."

I remain quiet as I listen to the details that Diane believes to be true. She goes on and on about Cal not being emotionally available for Sara, working too much, dragging his feet about getting married, and even not wanting to purchase my house. I'm amazed that my house continues to be such an important factor in Cal and Sara's relationship. It's not surprising that Diane is placing the sole blame on Cal for the breakup.

"I'm sorry Sara is having such a hard day. Please let her know that I'm not upset about them leaving the dinner last night. Obviously, they had more pressing matters to deal with."

"I told her that," she insists. "The poor thing is so distraught this morning. She thinks that you and she won't be friends after this because you knew Calvin in high school, which is nonsense. I tried to tell her that it doesn't matter. I only talk to one person I went to high school with."

I purse my lips.

I don't have anything against Sara as a person. Honestly, I barely know her, and we haven't had a lot of time to form a solid friendship. At the same time, I tend to keep my circle of close friends small. Gabby is one of my best friends, and she's engaged to Theo who happens to be Cal's best friend. The odds are that I'd support Cal, despite the history we share.

"Sara's coming over for lunch. Are you free? Can you come and talk to her?"

I groan silently as she gives me every reason in the universe that Sara needs people to rally around her right now. Seriously, she just met me. Doesn't she have any other friends?

Gabby walks outside with a box of Lucky Charms, two bowls, and two spoons. That's a genius idea, I could definitely use some of that cereal right now.

"Who's on the phone?" she whispers.

"Diane," I mouth.

Her mouth drops open, and I roll my eyes.

"I wish I could come, but I have a full day today," I lie. She doesn't need to know that I'm sitting by my pool in my pajamas.

"Oh, I understand ... What about dinner?"

Ugh. She's going to keep asking until I say yes. I know the drill after working with her for all those months. This isn't how I expected to spend my Sunday.

"Let me see if I can switch some things around," I tell her. "Can I get back to you in a little while?"

I'm planning to come up with a great reason not to go to dinner.

"Definitely. I'm still waiting to hear back from Sara. She was on her way to Calvin's to get some of her things and to try to talk to him."

A knot begins to twist in my stomach.

"Oh, well, maybe they will work things out," I suggest.

Cal wouldn't give her another chance, would he?

"I'm very hopeful, but I don't know."

I promise Diane that I will get back to her and hurry to get off the phone.

"She wants you to come over?" Gabby asks.

"Yes, to have lunch or dinner and talk to Sara," I say, placing my hands on my head. "How did this become my problem? I've only known that girl for a few weeks."

"Diane considers you part of her family, remember?" she reminds me. "You worked tirelessly to get them that house."

"And she thinks of Sara like a daughter," I add. "Although, who knows what's going to happen. Sara went to see Cal this morning. Maybe they'll get back together."

Gabby makes a face. "No way. Theo says they are done for good."

Theo doesn't know everything, even though he thinks he does.

"Sara didn't tell Diane the truth," I exclaim. 'She put all the blame on Cal, so of course Diane thinks he's a monster who broke her niece's heart."

Gabby shrugs. "Well maybe you should set her straight."

I purse my lips together. "Maybe I should."

Gabby pours the cereal into our bowls, and we eat while chatting. I change the subject and ask her if Theo and she have talked about wedding plans.

"We have." A look of panic spreads across her face.

I put my hand on hers. "Calm down. This isn't like last time."

She nods. "I know, I know. We want to do something simple on the beach with our closest friends and family followed by an intimate dinner."

"That sounds perfect."

She nods. "I was planning a big wedding last time, and part of that was for my family. This day is about Theo and me, no one else."

"Exactly ... I love the intimate dinner idea."

She inhales deeply. "I was going to talk to you and Reagan about this later, but I may as well ask now. Would you be interested in being one of my bridesmaids? It will just be you and Reagan, and my sister-in-law. I wouldn't even know Theo if it wasn't for you."

All of a sudden, a rush of emotion shoots through me as I nod and fight back tears. "I'm sorry I gave you such a hard time about Theo in the beginning," I say, dropping my head. "I was being selfish because I was mad at him."

"It's doesn't matter."

"Yes, it does," I insist. "I'm glad you didn't listen to me."

She laughs. "Yeah, I didn't know how that was going to turn out."

"Thank you for asking me. I'd be honored to be a part of your day." I pause. "Mrs. Theo Jorgenson ... are you sure?"

We both start laughing.

"I'll make Theo call Cal," she says. "That way we'll know what's happening, and you can decide if you want to go have dinner with them."

She runs into the house to get her phone. I put my cereal bowl down on the table and stare out at my backyard. Is there a chance that Cal and Sara get back together? Ew. The thought makes me sick to my stomach.

"Diane Hillard told Lila that Sara was over at Cal's," Gabby says into the phone.

"A few minutes ago."

She grits her teeth and holds up her phone. Theo is calling him now.

"What did he say?"

"He said that Cal will never take her back, just like I told you."

I sigh. "We'll see."

Reagan comes home from brunch with Jeremy, and we fill her in on everything that happened when Cal came over late last night and Diane's phone call. Gabby asks Reagan to be a bridesmaid in her wedding and Reagan cries, a lot. After she finally calms down, I make her cry again by asking if they want to find a new place to rent together.

"I thought you might move in with Theo," I tell Gabby.

She shakes her head. "We talked about it, but we want to wait until we're married so we can officially start that part of our life together."

"I think that makes it more special," Reagan says.

"I'm going to miss him being right next door though," Gabby says, her face falling.

I pretend to roll my eyes. "You'll survive for a few months."

Gabby's phone rings, and she dives for it. Reagan and I sit on the edge of our seats while we wait to get the scoop.

"Hey."

She's quiet as she listens.

I hold up my hands. "What's happening?"

She holds up her finger. "No way," she exclaims. Damn, I should've told her to put the speaker on.

"Okay, I'll tell Lila. Love you."

"What did he say?" Reagan shouts before she has a chance to end the call.

Her eyes grow wide. "Apparently, Sara went over there and was begging Cal to take her back. After he said no, they had a huge blowup, and she was furious. She was throwing his things around the house and completely lost it."

"Oh, wow."

I guess Sara isn't as sweet as Diane thinks she is.

"Cal was heading to his parents' house, but Theo invited him to his house later."

I lean back on the couch and exhale.

"There's no way I'm going to Diane's," I announce. "I won't be able to sit there and listen to Sara play victim all night."

"Yeah, you should stay away," Reagan agrees. "At least until the dust settles."

I shoot Diane a quick text letting her know that I wasn't able to switch my schedule and asked for a rain check. I refuse to get dragged into a mess that has nothing to do with me. I'm glad Cal is going to his parents' house. If anyone can comfort him, it's his mom.

Chapter Eighteen

Despite my lazy morning, I end up having a productive day. I find two condos and a house for my roommates and me that I go to look at. I also leave a message for my parents, letting them know that I'm finally ready to move forward with listing the house. They told me I had time, but why prolong the inevitable? It's not going to get any easier, and at least now I know I'll still be able to live with Reagan, and Gabby until she gets married. Of course Cal has been in the back of my mind the whole day.

Diane finally texted me back and asked me about coming to dinner later in the week. I told her I'd let her know. I won't be able to avoid her forever, but I'll try for as long as possible.

"Are you sure you don't want to come with me to Kennedy's house?" Reagan asks, as she digs around in her handbag.

I sigh. "You know I adore your sister, but I think I'm going to stay home tonight."

She presses her lips together and tries to hide her smile.

"What?" I ask.

"Nothing."

"Just say what you're thinking."

"I was just thinking that if Cal goes to Theo's, then you could pop next door and check in on him."

I wrinkle my nose. "I don't *ever* pop over to Theo Jorgenson's house."

She giggles. "I thought you two were getting to be close friends."

"Whoa"—I hold up my hands to stop her—"Let's not get ahead of ourselves. We're still learning how to be in the same room with each other."

"I heard that," Gabby calls from the kitchen.

"You know what I mean," I reply.

Reagan leaves, and Gabby sits down next to me on the couch.

"Why don't you just come over to Theo's with me?"

I shake my head. "Because it's weird. Cal just broke up with Sara, and it'll look like I'm trying to …"

"To what? Be his friend? How dare you!" she says dramatically.

I'm still trying to get used to the idea that I'm friends with Cal and Theo after all these years.

"Okay, if he brings it up, maybe I'll come over. But you have to promise me that you won't initiate it."

"I promise."

"I'll be really mad."

Her eyes widen. "Yikes. I definitely don't want that."

"Hey. I think I'm getting nicer in my old age."

She laughs loudly. "That's what Theo said."

I scowl. Maybe I need to reconsider this newfound friendship we have going on.

Gabby leaves a few minutes later, and I try to make myself busy. I'm probably being really stupid. Ugh, sometimes I think Cal Sims brings out a different, vulnerable side of me. That's definitely not something I'm used to.

∾

I'm completely zoning out when a knock on one of the french doors makes me jump up in the air. When I get up to check, I see Cal waving to me through the glass.

"Hey. What are you doing here?" I ask, opening the door.

"I came to invite you to Theo's."

I frown. "Did Gabby make you come over here? What did she say?"

He holds up his hands innocently. "It was all my idea. She just said that Reagan went to her sister's and you were here alone working."

"That's all?"

He nods. "Yep."

He leans against the door frame. "So, can you pull yourself away from work for an hour? Please don't leave me alone with the lovebirds."

I sigh. "Come on in while I get my shoes."

I run to my room and quickly check myself in the mirror.

You're friends, Lila. There's no need to check your reflection.

I'm wearing a simple, black, cropped T-shirt and jeans and my hair is falling loosely down my back. At least it's an improvement from the faded flannel pajamas I was wearing last night.

Cal is sitting on my couch with his feet up when I come out. I can't help but notice how good he looks in his white T-shirt and gray joggers.

Ugh. Pull it together, Lila.

"How are you feeling today?" I ask. "Did you have to work?"

He shakes his head. "I'm back on shift tomorrow, and I'm doing okay."

I sit down on the couch and slip into my flip-flops.

"My mom says hi, by the way."

Hmm … I guess that means they were discussing me.

"She's the sweetest lady," I say.

"I have to agree."

Neither of us says anything for a few seconds.

"I'm ready when you are," I announce. "Let's go to Theo's."

Those are words I never thought I'd be saying.

As soon as I stand up, Cal stops me by putting his hand on my arm.

"Lila, I wanted to thank you for listening last night."

"Of course," I say, clearing my throat. "I was happy to help."

We're standing a few inches apart, which is making my heart pound against my chest. Our gazes lock and I feel dizzy from the invisible pull that's happening between us.

What the hell am I doing? He just broke up with his girlfriend not even twenty-four hours ago. I won't be a rebound for any man, not even Cal Sims.

"We should probably go," I say.

We walk through my backyard in silence, but I'm still thinking about the moment we just had. There have been a few since we reconnected, except this time he's single.

Once we're safely inside his house, Gabby and Theo do a great job of breaking the ice. Theo ordered pizza and breadsticks from Slices and Salads, the best pizza shop in town. He's really pulling out all the stops to win me over.

"Maybe we should find a movie to watch," Gabby suggests.

"Fine, but no horror or end of world stuff," I say, popping a piece of pepperoni into my mouth.

"Boo," Theo whines.

"I think Cal should choose the movie," Gabby says. That's fair considering the purpose of this night is to cheer Cal up.

"I like that idea," he agrees.

"All right, man, what's your choice?" Theo asks, reaching for the remote control.

He pauses and gives a thoughtful look. "Let's watch 'Never Been Kissed' with Drew Barrymore."

Wait, what? That's my favorite movie. I make every effort not to show any emotion, but inside I'm dying. I can't believe he actually remembered.

Gabby shoots me a glance.

"Great movie," I say nonchalantly.

"Seriously?" Theo exclaims. "Of all the movies ever made you choose that one. Come on, man."

"I think it's a good idea," Gabby insists.

Theo begrudgingly searches through the list of movies. Obviously he has no idea what's going on, and I'm a little confused myself.

We all stretch out on Theo's huge sectional couch. Of course Theo and Gabby are snuggling close together on one end, while Cal and I are sitting in the two recliners with a console between us on the other end.

I laugh through all the funny parts of the movie, but my mind is a million miles away. I'm trying desperately not to overthink what's happening with Cal and me. Gabby made a great point about me being Cal's friend. Obviously this casual night of pizza and movies is about supporting him and giving him something to do after his breakup. Yes, he chose to watch my favorite movie, but that doesn't mean he's ready to embark on a romance with me. And when I ended things with Jordan, I committed to taking a break from relationships and being on my own for a while. I'm not planning to go back on that.

All of the sudden Theo pauses the movie, which drags me out of my thoughts.

"Ugh. This movie is so embarrassing. Who wants ice cream?" He jumps up from the couch and heads to the kitchen.

Gabby shrugs her shoulders and then follows him.

Neither Cal nor I move from our recliners.

He turns his head to face me. "Thanks for coming and not leaving me alone with the happy couple."

I smile. "No problem. Did you really want to watch this movie, or did you just want to annoy Theo?"

"Both, but mostly to annoy him."

"I love it." I hold up my hand to give him a high five. His hand touches mine, but he doesn't pull it away. His fingers slowly curl around mine. Our gazes lock once again, but this time I don't look away. He starts to move his face closer to mine, and just as he reaches for my cheek, Theo returns like a bull in a china shop.

"Guys, we have—oh, damn, sorry."

Gabby appears right behind him, her jaw dropping open.

"I actually think I will get some ice cream," I announce. "I've already had pizza, so what the hell."

I kick the recliner closed and hurry to the kitchen. Thankfully, Gabby reads my mind and joins me.

"What—"

I hold up my hand to stop her from saying another word.

"I don't know what I'm doing, but I need to stop it," I whisper.

"Why?"

"Are you kidding me? Why do you think? He's just barely single, and the last thing I need is to get involved with Cal Sims all over again. We're not teenagers anymore."

Of course my brain is telling me one thing, but my heart is saying another.

"I understand... But is that what you really want?"

I twist my hair around my fingers. "It has to be."

"The Lila Barlow I know takes risks and doesn't hide from things."

I sigh. "That's true, but this is different."

"Because it's him."

"Yes."

She laughs as I reach for the carton of Rocky Road.

"By the way, your fiancé has the worst timing ever."

She laughs. "You know you love him like a brother."

"Yep. I always said he's like the brother I never wanted."

I add a scoop of ice cream to a small bowl.

"Maybe you just need to have fun tonight," she suggests. "And let things happen naturally."

That's exactly what I'm afraid of, but she's right. I need to just relax and be myself.

I bring my ice cream back to the living room to find Theo sitting in my seat, whispering to Cal.

"Okay, break it up," I announce. "You're in my seat, Jorgenson."

He laughs as he stands up. "You haven't called me that in years."

"Probably because I haven't talked to you in years." I wink at Cal as I reclaim my seat.

"Yeah, you used to be really mean," Theo says, moving back to his seat next to Gabby.

"Well, you deserved it."

He nods. "I know, and I was wrong for assuming the worst about you and Brent."

I glance at Cal who is eyeing me curiously.

"I've forgiven you for that. I know everything happens for a reason."

"I'm sad you're not going to be my neighbor anymore," he says softly.

"Me too."

The craziest thing is that I actually mean it. I'm going to miss living next door more than I ever thought I would.

"Aw, you guys are going to make me cry," Gabby wails.

After all these years I think we can finally put this subject to rest. It's time to move forward and be ready for what comes next.

Chapter Nineteen

We finally finish watching the movie, despite Theo's complaints about all the secondhand embarrassment. When I announce that I need to get home, Cal asks if he can walk with me, making my stomach do a nervous flip. I appreciate his chivalry, but it's not like I'm walking down a deserted street in the middle of the city.

We thank Theo for hosting and set out on our long trek right next door. We're both quiet as we walk, so I decide to break the silence first. "I can't believe I admitted that I was going to miss living next door to Theo."

"Yeah, that surprised me too," he says.

"I only did it for Gabby," I insist.

"Absolutely, because you're a good friend."

We both start to laugh.

He clears his throat. "Lila, about what happened over there—"

"Don't worry about it."

He stops me before we reach my door. "I just don't want you to think I did that because I'm on the rebound … I've really enjoyed spending time with you lately."

Here we go, sometimes honesty is the best policy.

"I feel the same, but you just broke up with Sara last night," I remind him.

"Yeah…"

"So maybe you need some time to get used to life without her."

He opens his mouth and then closes it quickly.

"Three years is a long time to be with someone," I add.

I feel like this conversation is as much for me as it is for him.

"Will you have dinner with me?" he asks, sliding closer to me. "As friends."

What the hell? Did he not hear a word I just said? His blue eyes are burning into mine, and I feel like I'm having déjà vu. It's highly likely that we've stood in this same spot before.

"As friends," I repeat softly.

"Yes."

Suddenly I have the urge to wrap my arms around his neck and pull his lips to mine, which goes against everything I just said.

Don't do it, Lila.

"Unless you don't trust yourself around me," he adds, the corner of his mouth curling up.

Um, what? The urge I just had is halted by his overconfidence.

"Oh, I don't think you want to go there," I say.

He gives a casual shrug and places his on hand on the door frame next to me. "Are you up for the challenge? It's just two old friends eating a meal together."

This is the Cal Sims I remember. Smooth, calm, and confident.

"I'm always up for a challenge," I reply. "So, it's a yes."

He smiles proudly. "Next weekend?"

"Fine."

He slides his hand down the door frame. "I'll be in touch. Good night, Lila."

He turns around and walks back into the dark yard toward Theo's house.

I wait a few minutes before going inside. I have no idea what just happened, but somehow I've agreed to dinner with Cal. My eighteen-year-old self is ecstatic about this second chance, but the present day me is wondering if I'm opening a door that should remain closed.

∼

One of the reasons I love Pilates is the chance to be active, to focus and relax. And I've met some great people in my classes, like Reagan.

I'm stretching out on my mat with my eyes closed when Reagan groans loudly.

"Lila," she whispers.

"Good morning, ladies," a shrill voice says.

I open one eye to see Bethany standing over me. This is not the way I wanted to start my day. Hopefully it's not an omen of things to come. She's wearing a gray snakeskin-printed sports bra with matching leggings and a full face of makeup. Has this girl ever taken an advanced Pilates class? This should be quite entertaining.

"I forgot you came to this studio," she says, pretending to be shocked.

Lies, all lies.

"Bethany," Reagan says, her voice strained. "What are you doing here?"

I continue my stretching without saying anything.

"It's good to see you too, Reagan," she says with a giggle.

I'm not sure what she thinks is so funny. I guess she's oblivious to the fact that we're not happy to see her this early, or ever.

"I've heard this is the best place to take yoga and Pilates, so I thought I'd give it a try."

I open my eyes and shoot Reagan a glance. It might be time for us to switch studios.

"Reagan, I never heard back from you about getting together," she whines. "I know you were pretty upset the last time we talked."

"Do you mean when you told her that I was selling my house?" I say, without opening my eyes. I have nothing to lose, and I'm usually someone who gets right to the point.

"Well, it's not my fault you weren't being honest with your roommates."

I inhale deeply followed by an exhale. "It shouldn't be any concern of yours, considering it has nothing to do with you," I reply sharply.

I continue to concentrate on my breathing in order to keep myself calm.

"Reagan is my oldest and dearest friend, so that makes it my concern."

This girl is unbelievable.

I'm about to mention Jordan, when our instructor comes in to start the class. Of course Bethany lays out her mat on the other side of Reagan because she can't take a hint, ever. Thankfully there's no more talking for the next hour.

During my practice, I zone out and let my mind wander. I have enough to think about without letting stupid Bethany take any of my energy. My home is going up for sale, I need to talk to Elizabeth about her offer to run Fun in the Sun, and I'm having dinner with Cal in a few days—as friends. I'm the type of person who thrives when things are chaotic, so I should be able to handle everything with grace. I hope.

"I really enjoyed that workout," Bethany says as soon as the lights come on. "Reagan, do you remember when we took that hip hop class back in Chicago? We had a such a blast, even though hip hop isn't really my thing. I was terrible."

A smile spreads across Reagan's face. "It wasn't really my thing either, but I wanted it to be. I gave it my best effort though."

"Me too," she squeals.

Ugh. Somehow I've ended up in the middle of a trip down memory lane with Bethany. The last place I want to be.

"Do you gals usually get coffee or breakfast after class?" Bethany asks. "We should go grab something."

Honestly, I think this girl lives in an alternate universe. A few weeks ago she reached out to Bethany to throw me under the bus, and now she wants to have coffee like we're all the best of friends. Maybe things could be different if she didn't always have an ulterior motive. And if she really just wants to be friends with Reagan again, she went about it the wrong way by telling her about the house sale.

"Sorry, I have to get to a meeting," I say, not sounding sorry at all.

I take my phone out of my bag and find a text message from Diane.

I've managed to avoid her since the weekend, claiming I was busy, but I can't do it forever. I just know she's going to want to talk about Sara and Cal, and I don't.

Reagan and Bethany are still chatting about the hip hop class.

"Lila, I'm sorry about telling Reagan about the house. You were right, it probably wasn't my place. Sometimes I get overprotective because she's looked out for me most of my life."

I do an internal eye roll.

"I actually understand that because I can be overprotective too," I reply. "I care about Jordan, so I hope you're not playing games with him like you did with Paul."

Her mouth drops open. "Paul and I were always just friends, and he knew that."

I hold up my hands. "I'm just being protective of my friends—like you."

She purses her lips together but doesn't say anything for a few seconds.

"Jordan is a really nice person," she says softly.

Ugh. Why am I detecting some sincerity from her?

"Yes, he is," I agree.

"And you broke up with him."

She has a point. I did break up with Jordan, but that doesn't mean I don't care about him.

"Jordan is free to date whomever he wants, but I don't want to see him hurt."

I could get into a long discussion about Bethany's track record since she first came to Miami to visit. At first she had her sights on Dante the chef, mostly to get back at Reagan, but when he didn't reciprocate her feelings, she latched onto Paul. She used him for a while to meet people in town and find a job. So, my doubts about her liking Jordan are well supported.

I check the time. "I need to get going. I'll see you tonight, Reagan."

When I get in my car, I respond to Diane's text.

Sorry for the delay. Been so busy. Let's catch up this evening.

I'm not sure how the conversation is going to go, but I can't avoid it forever. I usually face things head on, so there's no reason to stop now.

Chapter Twenty

I'm sitting in Elizabeth's office waiting for her to finish her phone call. She appears frazzled despite looking so much better after making her decision to move to London. The dark circles under her eyes have returned, and her clothes are wrinkled again.

"Are you okay?" I ask after she ends her call.

She shakes her head. "I'm having so many doubts about picking up my whole life and moving across the pond. Even Billy is starting to second guess his decision."

I frown. "Well, you're probably not going to like what I have to say."

"You don't want to take over the agency, do you?"

I shake my head. "I'm sorry. I gave it some thought, but I don't think it's a good fit for my life right now."

She lets out a heavy sigh. "I had a feeling, but I wanted to give it a shot. It's a lot to take on."

"I'm so flattered that you would trust me enough with this agency," I continue.

She nods. "You've been my star for as long as I can remember."

I give her a grateful smile. "Are you sure you can't run it from a far, at least until you get settled?"

"I'm thinking about it," she says. "I'm so worried that we're going to get over there and hate it. And what if we decide that we want to come back? I don't want to give all of this up until I'm sure."

All of a sudden an idea pops into my head. "You could ask Gabby to help oversee things while you're gone. She has as much experience in the industry as I do, if not more. And if there's one person you can count on, it's her."

She gives a thoughtful look. "I didn't think about asking Gabby."

"You know she's struggled a bit since moving to Miami."

She nods. "I know. I've talked to my sister about it."

I don't tell Elizabeth that Gabby has thought about leaving real estate to start something new. I know she enjoyed planning Theo's party, but I believe her heart is in real estate. Maybe this is a way to help her and Elizabeth in the meantime.

"I'll talk to her about it ... Thank you for being such a good friend to Gabby. Nikki was so worried about her after what happened back in Orlando."

"I was just telling Gabby that I think I've become a nicer person over time, maybe she's rubbing off on me."

She laughs. "Well, you said it."

After I leave Elizabeth's office, I'm feeling proud of myself. She already seemed a bit more relaxed than when I first arrived.

When Gabby arrives, I can't help but feel excited. I hope my idea works out and benefits both her and Elizabeth.

Without fail, Diane Hillard calls me at five o'clock sharp. I did tell her we'd catch up this evening, but I haven't even left the office yet.

"Hello, Diane," I say politely.

"Hi. I'm so glad to finally talk to you because I'm in desperate need of your help," she says, her voice panicked.

"I'll try my best."

"Do you have dinner plans?"

For some reason my dinner with Cal pops into my head, but I know that's not what she's referring to.

"Um, not tonight."

"Would you like to come over? I have a roast in the crockpot, and it's too much food for just Dave and me."

I might as well get this over with, and a roast does sound delicious.

"Sure. I haven't left the office yet, but I can be there within a half hour."

"Oh, that would be terrific. We'll see you soon."

"Can I bring anything?" I offer.

"Just yourself."

When I hang up the phone, I sigh. I already know how this evening is going to go, so I send Cal a quick text.

FYI. Having dinner at the Hillards'. Will keep you posted.

He's been on shift at the hospital for the last few days, so I haven't spoken to him other than a quick text about dinner on Friday. It's actually none of his business if I go to the Hillards', but considering the situation with Sara, I want to keep him in the loop.

~

As soon as I pull into Diane's driveway, my phone rings. My heart skips a beat when I see Cal's number on the screen.

"Hey."

"Hi, is it safe?"

I laugh. "I just pulled up, so yes," I say. "Is there anything I need to know before I go in there?"

He groans. "Sara has called me a few times, but I haven't spoken to her."

"Oh, well, maybe you should talk to her."

"There's nothing left to say," he replies flatly. "I saw AJ at the hospital yesterday, and it just reminded me that I made the right decision. It also reminded me that I should've listened to my mother a long time ago."

"Did your mom tell you to end things?"

"Not in so many words," he says. "She dropped plenty of hints, but you know her. She tries to be kind to everyone."

"Yes. She's probably the nicest person on the planet," I say. "We should all try to be more like her."

"Anyway, Diane and David are really nice people," he says. "I'm sorry if my problems make things awkward for you."

"It'll be fine. I can handle it."

"Okay, good luck."

"Thanks."

"Lila."

"Yes."

"I'm looking forward to Friday night," he says eagerly.

"Me too. Bye."

"Bye."

Oh, Lila. What are you getting yourself into?

The door flies open, and Diane pulls me in for one of her signature hugs.

"I'm so glad you could come," she exclaims. "Wait until you see all the house projects we've been working on."

I'm actually excited to see the work they've done on the house. I do love a good home renovation.

Diane is wearing a pink T-shirt, denim capris, and more of those hideous rubber/plastic shoes. A good friend would tell her how tragic the shoes are, but I'm already going to be walking a fine line. Then she starts talking about Sara and Cal.

"Dave is out running some errands, so we have some time for girl talk."

"Great. I love girl talk," I lie. "I'd love to see what you've done in the house first."

Maybe I can keep her occupied with that for a while.

She leads me to the guest bath where she's added some floral wallpaper. Normally I would be against floral, but the print she's chosen isn't completely unsightly. She's added some floating shelves with towels, and it actually looks nice. If anything, it's very Diane, bright and cheerful.

"Can I get you a drink? A Mountain Dew?"

I force a smile. Not a chance. "I'm okay right now. Thanks."

"David doesn't love the wallpaper, but we made a deal, and I gave him free rein over the office."

"That sounds like a fair trade."

We continue on our tour, and she takes me to one of the rooms where she's adding book shelving and a window seat.

"I thought this could be a fun room for younger guests," she pauses, her face falling. "I had this dream of Sara and Cal having a child and they'd come stay with their aunt Diane on weekends."

Ugh. And here we go. I'm sure this is hard for her because she thinks of Sara as a daughter.

"I'm sorry, Diane."

She presses her lips together and places her hands on her chest.

"It's just hard because I know Sara is so devastated. This breakup came out of nowhere. She was completely blindsided."

No, what's really hard is that she doesn't know the whole story. I certainly don't want to be the one to destroy the image she has of Sara.

Diane leads me to the kitchen, where she checks on the roast. As soon as she lifts the lid, an intoxicating aroma fills the air. The smell alone was worth this awkward visit.

"Did Sara tell you exactly what happened?"

"You were there, weren't you?" she asks. "It happened at your house."

Oh, I was there all right. She and AJ disappeared together, and Cal found them.

"Anyway, Sara will tell you more when she gets here."

Sara's coming? Lovely. I should've known.

"Hi, Aunt Diane."

I didn't even have enough time to gather my thoughts before she arrives.

When Sara comes into the kitchen. She immediately runs to me and gives me a hug.

"Lila, I'm glad you could come over. I've been wanting to reach out to you, but Aunt Diane suggested it would be better if we could talk in person."

"Hey, Sara, how are you?"

Normally I'm not the best at hiding my feelings, but I'll put on my best acting skills for Diane's sake.

"I've been better," she says sadly. "I'm sure you've heard the news. Gabby probably thinks I'm a terrible person too."

I shake my head. "You know Gabby. She minds her own business."

Diane pours glasses of water for Sara and me after we both decline the Mountain Dew.

"I was just telling Lila that you could explain what happened after you and Calvin left her house."

"Yes, it happened so abruptly I'm still a little confused about the details." I look Sara straight in the eyes. I'm interested to hear the spin she puts on the story.

She launches into the fight that she and Cal had been having about a few things, including the purchase of my home. It's the same story that Cal explained.

"When he stormed out of your house, I followed him. That's when he told me that he'd been having doubts for a while and didn't think he loved me anymore." She stops and gulps. "Can you believe it, after I gave him three years of my life?"

"I'm so disappointed in him," Diane snaps. "I never expected this kind of behavior from him, of all people."

"But I think there's more to the story," Sara says, lowering her voice. "I think he has feelings for someone else and he's using the excuse that we've grown apart. And blaming me for the cracks in our relationship."

Her expression has quickly changed, and she's eyeing me with pure disgust.

"Oh, honey, I doubt that," Diane calls from the stove. "I think he got cold feet when you asked him about moving in together. He's been stalling for a while."

Sara finally lifts her gaze off of me.

"Oh, Aunt Diane, I picked up some of those pastries you love. I forgot them in my car."

"I can grab them," Diane offers.

That was a clever way to get Diane to leave us alone. If Sara really wants to have this conversation, I'm ready.

As soon as Diane leaves the room, Sara turns on me. "Consider this a warning. Don't think for a second that you can just move in and claim Cal," she sneers, her voice barely above a whisper.

I raise my eyebrows. "Why do you care what Cal does? You tossed him aside when you hooked up with Dr. Bennett. Very interesting that you left that part out when you were giving Aunt Diane your sob story."

She glares at me. "Just because you dated him a for a minute when you were a teenager doesn't mean you have another chance now. Cal and I will eventually find our way back to each other."

"These look delicious," Diane calls, interrupting us. "Thank you, sweetie."

She holds open a box of pastries to me.

"No, thank you."

Sara definitely has everyone fooled. Dare I say, she makes Bethany look like a girl scout?

When Diane mentions Cal again, Sara tells her that she doesn't want to talk about it anymore because it's too difficult. And of course Diane falls for it hook, line, and sinker.

I plaster a smile on my face as we talk about house ideas and the real estate market. Somehow I manage to get through dinner and escape before dessert is served.

On my way home, I replay the conversation Sara and I had. The doubts are creeping in, and I'm starting to think dinner with Cal is a bad idea. Maybe it's too soon, and as much as I want to believe he and I can only be friends, I'm just not sure.

Chapter Twenty-One

I've always thought of myself as resilient, strong willed, and tough. But like everyone, I have those hard days when all my insecurities creep up to the surface and consume me. My issue is that I've never been comfortable showing this side of myself. Anytime it happens, I dig my heels in deeper and put all my focus into things I can control, like my job or anything that will keep me focused so I don't have to feel.

"What do you mean, you're canceling your dinner?" Reagan shouts.

It's Friday morning, and I'm standing in my kitchen making a protein shake. Reagan and I just got home from Pilates class, without Bethany, thankfully.

"There's just a lot going on," I reply. "We need to get this house listed, and my mother sent me a list of projects. And there's a stack of boxes in the garage that I need to look through."

Reagan rushes off without a word, and I roll my eyes. She returns with Gabby, whose hair is wrapped up in a towel.

"What's going on? Why would you cancel dinner?"

I sit down on one of the bar stools. "It's just bad timing."

"You're listening to Sara, aren't you?" Gabby accuses. "You can't let her get in your head."

"I'm not," I mutter. "Cal's only been single for a week. We have plenty of time to have dinner together."

"Why are you worried about it? I thought you were having dinner as friends," Reagan says pointedly.

"We are—we were."

"Do I need to call Theo?" Gabby asks.

I make a face. "Why would you do that?"

"To talk some sense into you."

I roll my eyes. "Look, Gabby, you know how hard I've tried to be friends with your fiancé. Asking him to talk to me isn't going to make me do something."

"No, but he will tell you how much Cal is looking forward to tonight and how he's brought it up every time he's talked to him this week."

"Aw ... don't disappoint him," Reagan wails. "I'll help you go through the boxes in the garage tomorrow."

"Sara is the one who cheated on Cal," Gabby reminds me. "Don't let her win by not having dinner with him."

I sigh. These two are a force to be reckoned with when they band together, and I'm supposed to be the tough one.

"Fine," I say. "You guys love ganging up on me, don't you?"

They both laugh.

"You'd do the same for us," Reagan says.

"You *have* done the same for us," Gabby adds. "That's what makes us such a good team."

"We're like the three musketeers," Gabby suggests.

I hold up my hand. "Nope. No cheesy nicknames."

She giggles. "I knew you were going to say that."

"Now that the crisis is averted, I have to finish getting ready," Gabby says. "Elizabeth asked to meet with me this morning."

I try to hide my smile because I know what that meeting is about.

She rushes back to her room leaving Reagan and me alone.

"You sure you're okay?" she asks.

I scoff. "Of course. You can leave me alone. I promise I'm not going to skip the country or anything."

She throws her arm around my shoulder and gives it a squeeze before heading off to get ready for her day.

It's moments like this that add to my sadness when I think about moving out of here. This house is what brought the three of us together, and at the time I was just in search of two roommates. I honestly never thought I'd be so blessed to gain two amazing friends like Gabby and Reagan. At least I know our friendship will go on no matter where we are living or what direction our lives take us in.

∽

Dinner with an old friend. What would be considered appropriate attire for an evening like this? Honestly, I'm not worrying about it because I'm going to wear what I'm comfortable in. I choose a pair of black flared jeans with a cream waffle-knit sweater. I add some loose curls to my hair and throw on a pair of black booties.

Neither Gabby nor Reagan are here, but they both checked on me to make sure I didn't get cold feet. Gabby mentioned that her meeting with Elizabeth went very well, but she had to rush off the phone. I'd say that's a good sign.

I'm just adding perfume to my wrists when I hear the doorbell.

I saunter to the door casually. Although in my mind I'm running to answer it like I did when I was seventeen.

When I open the door, Cal is waiting with his hands shoved in his pockets.

For a brief moment, I have a flashback. It isn't often that the same man picks you up for dinner in the same place nearly ten years apart.

"Hey, friend," Cal teases.

I try not to laugh, but I'm unsuccessful. "Come in," I say, holding the door open. "You're really going to emphasize the *friend* thing tonight, aren't you?"

He shrugs. "I was planning on it—unless you think it's too much."

"Maybe once an hour will suffice."

"Deal."

He stops as soon as he steps into the foyer and pulls me towards him, wrapping his arms around me.

"I decided against bringing flowers. So a hug will have to do."

I rest my cheek against his chest and breathe in his delicious masculine scent.

"Contrary to popular opinion, I'm not big on flowers," I say, hugging him back.

He doesn't let go for a few seconds, and I don't pull away either.

"What a relief. I almost called Gabby to check, but I went with my gut instead."

When we pull away, he keeps his hands on my waist.

"I'm not even sure friends are supposed to bring flowers," I say, raising an eyebrow.

"I thought about that too."

He links his hands against my lower back while I run my hands over his broad shoulders.

My mind begins to wander into places it shouldn't be, so I quickly move away from him and head to the kitchen to grab my bag.

"So, where are we having dinner?" I ask.

He places his hands on the counter.

"Well, there's a quick stop we have to make before we eat. If that's okay?"

I give him a concerned look. "That depends on where it is?"

He shrugs and turns around to walk toward the door. "You'll see."

My eyes inadvertently move down to how good he looks in his jeans.

Gah. I'm in big trouble.

It's been years since I've been to this house, and it looks exactly the same. When we pull up in front of Cal's parents' house, I'm speechless.

"I hope you don't mind, but my mom asked if we'd stop by."

Friends, Lila. You're friends.

"I don't mind at all."

We get out of the car, and I walk up the cobblestone path toward the front door. As soon as we're inside, I'm hit with a familiar smell that has been etched in my brain for years. I recall that Mrs. Sims always had candles burning.

As we walk through the house, I see that the walls are covered with pictures of Cal and his older brother, Kevin, when they were kids. The house has had updates with paints and furniture, but the warm, welcoming vibe is still present. There's a massive family picture on the wall that must've been taken at his brother's wedding and tons of pictures of an adorable baby girl.

"That's my niece. Isn't she the cutest thing you've ever seen?" Cal says when he notices me looking at the photos.

I nod. Admittedly I'm looking around to see if I spot any photos with Sara, but so far there isn't a trace of her. Maybe Mrs. Sims already cleaned house?

"Hey, Mom," Cal calls.

"We're in the office."

I follow Cal through the hallway to the office that's just to the left of the kitchen. All of a sudden another flashback hits me of us making out in this very office and his father walking in on us. I feel my face turn bright red at the memory.

As soon as we turn the corner, I see Cal's parents sitting together working on a puzzle. His father looks the same, only he's completely bald now.

"Look who came to visit," Cal announces.

Both Mrs. and Mr. Sims rise to their feet.

"Oh, what a nice surprise," Mrs. Sims says, although she doesn't seem surprised to see me at all. She gives me the same hug she gave me at Diane's birthday brunch, only this time it's even tighter.

"Dad, do you remember Lila Barlow from high school?"

His dad looks confused at first, but then a smile spreads across his face.

"Sure I do," he says. "It's about time, son."

Cal cringes while Mrs. Sims giggles nervously.

"It's nice to see you both," I say, ignoring his father's comment.

Mrs. Sims comments on how much she loves my outfit and how pretty my hair looks.

I soak up all the compliments and tell her how the house looks and smells the same.

She links her arm in mine and leads me to the living room to show me pictures of her granddaughter. Cal follows us without saying anything.

"Where are you kids off to?" Cal's dad asks, joining us in the living room. "You have plenty of gas in your car, right?"

He lets out the same jovial laugh he used to have.

Cal frowns again, while I burst out laughing.

"Oh, my goodness, I totally forgot about that night you ran out of gas."

He puts his hands on top of his forehead. "Yeah, and I had to call my dad to help us, which was so humiliating. No eighteen-year-old wants to call his dad when he's trying to impress the girl of his dreams."

A hush falls over the room.

"You know what I mean," Cal says quickly.

"Poor Cal was so embarrassed about it," his mother chimes in.

"To this day, I don't let my car get below a half a tank."

"It was a good lesson to learn," his dad says.

"So, are you just going to dinner or anywhere fun?" Mrs. Sims asks.

I look at Cal. "He hasn't told me yet."

"I have some stuff planned."

Cal's parents invite me to sit down and ask me all the questions about what I've been doing since high school. They were always easy to talk to, and this hasn't changed now that I'm an adult.

"I moved back to my parents' house with a few friends almost a year ago because I wasn't ready for them to sell it," I say. "Unfortunately, I was just prolonging the inevitable, and it's about to go on the market."

Mrs. Sims nods. I'm sure she remembers the big discussion about it at Diane's birthday party when Sara was trying to convince Cal to buy it for them.

Mrs. Sims sends Cal to the kitchen to get us some drinks. As soon as he's out of the room, she leans in close to me. "He's been talking about this evening for a week."

My pulse begins to pick up speed.

"Louise, don't give away his secrets," Cal's father scolds.

She waves her hand at her husband. "Oh, hush. I didn't say anything."

She turns back to me. "Anyway, I think it's great that you too are reconnecting. Did you know that Cal's father and I were high school sweethearts?"

"Louise."

"Mom, what are you saying?" Cal asks, returning with a few water bottles.

"I'm just chatting with Lila. Calm down."

I change the subject quickly and ask them about retirement life. Before I know it, Mrs. Sims has invited me to join her for Zumba. As much as I adore her, it would be a cold day in hell before I step foot in a Zumba class.

We chat for a few more minutes, and then Cal announces that he's starving. When we say our good-byes, his father reminds him again with a laugh to check his gas levels.

"You're welcome to come by anytime, even without Cal," Mrs. Sims says, squeezing my shoulders. "I know your parents are gone a lot, but we're always here."

For some reason this brings me an overwhelming feeling of comfort, and I just might have to take her up on the invitation, especially after my house no longer belongs to me.

Chapter Twenty-Two

Admittedly I've been on some very impressive dates in my life, from top-rated restaurants to private jets down to the Caribbean. But those actually don't compare to tonight. I can't remember the last time I laughed so much, and it feels fantastic. After we leave his parents' house, he tells me what he had planned. BBQ and miniature golf—which is actually exactly what we did on one of our first dates.

"How does that sound?" he asks.

"Perfect."

"I originally planned to wine and dine you, but I figured you're probably sick of that," he teases. "And friends do fun things together, like miniature golf."

I giggle. "It's perfect. I don't think I've played mini golf since the last time I went with you."

"Me neither," he says.

Our first stop is Babe's BBQ, which has amazing food. I don't know why my roommates and I don't order from here on a regular basis. I mentally add it to our takeout list.

Cal and I don't run out of things to talk about. We have a lot of years to catch up on, and by the end of dinner, it feels like we haven't missed a beat. The only subject we haven't discussed is Sara, and I'm fine with that. At the same time, I feel like it's the elephant in the room that's sitting there waiting to be addressed. He never asked me about dinner at Diane's, so he doesn't know about my less than pleasant run-in with Sara.

"Did you hear that Theo asked me to be his best man?"

I smile. "That sounds about right. Gabby asked Reagan and me to be bridesmaids."

He wipes the corners of his mouth with a napkin. "So, I guess I'll be seeing you at the wedding?"

I laugh. "I guess so."

He pushes his tray to the side. "Maybe we could go together—as friends, of course."

"Are you asking me to accompany you to the wedding? I don't think they've set a date yet."

He shrugs. "So?"

"I'm just saying that you might be swooped up by some hot nurse by then. News travels fast, and once it gets out that

Dr. Sims is available, there's no telling what kind of chaos will ensue. It could be like the bachelor—all those women fighting for one man."

He shakes his head. "I don't think so."

"I've heard what goes on in the medical field."

I've had plenty of friends who are nurses, and it sounds like it can get pretty wild.

"Maybe for some people, but that's not my thing," he says. "I've either been in school or in a committed relationship."

Meanwhile I've been a serial dater, although I don't say this out loud.

"So what do you think?" he asks, gazing at me with his piercing blue eyes. "Will you accompany me to Theo and Gabby's wedding?"

In general I have a lot of willpower, but it's slowly slipping away as the evening progresses. At this point I don't want this night to end, so planning another opportunity to spend time with Cal sounds good to me. "Sure. I'd like that."

After dinner we head to the same miniature golf place we used to go when we were younger which hasn't changed at all. It has the same waterfalls, bridges, and dark tunnels.

"Okay, Barlow, you might have won all those years ago, but it's time for a rematch," Cal says, placing the little blue golf ball down on the artificial turf.

"I'm prepared to win again," I say nonchalantly.

He pretends to study the distance and line up the ball before giving his club a gentle swing. The ball rolls and stops just short of the hole.

"Oh, what a shame. You gave it a good effort, though."

I place my pink ball down and hit it just right, the ball sails down the course and lands in the hole.

I cheer loudly, while Cal stares motionless.

"You can pull your jaw off the ground, doctor," I say as I walk by him.

It takes him two more tries to get his ball in the hole.

"Beginner's luck," Cal mutters.

I laugh. "What can I say? I like to win."

As we continue through the course, I'm totally kicking his butt. Who would've thought I'd be so good considering I haven't touched a golf club since I was a teenager? I can't help but notice that we're growing more and more comfortable with each other. At one point I place my hands on his hips to help him with his stance. And while we're waiting for another couple to finish at a hole, he wraps his arms around my shoulders and rests his chin on my head. Neither of us addresses the PDA. It just flows naturally like it was always supposed to be this way.

"Now this is my favorite part of the course," Cal says as he leads me through a series of dark tunnels to get to the next hole.

"Really, why?"

As soon as we're inside the tunnel, he stops walking and turns around to face me. I don't even have time to think before he lifts my chin with his finger and moves in to kiss me. As soon as his lips are on mine, all my worries and confusion vanish. I don't fight it or pull away. I drop my golf club and grab the collar of his shirt to pull him even closer to me—which isn't possible. He wraps his arms around my waist, not missing a beat on my lips.

Holy crap, I'm kissing Cal Sims in the middle of a mini golf course. And it's so freaking good.

"Excuse me," a voice says.

Cal and I manage to break free of one another and notice a family of four waiting to continue their game. The two young girls are staring at us with wide eyes, and their mother has a look of disgust on her face. I'm sure she was about to shield them from what they just interrupted.

"Sorry. You can go ahead of us," Cal says eagerly.

They rush past us, leaving us alone in the tunnel again.

"I'm actually not sorry," Cal whispers.

I smile. "Good, because neither am I."

"Do you think we'll get in trouble for making out in here?" he asks, pushing a strand of hair behind my ear.

"Maybe. Just as long as they don't call your dad."

He groans and throws his head back. "Why did you have to bring up my dad at a moment like this?"

I smile. "Well, someone has to be the responsible one, and we should probably keep moving before we scar more kids for life."

He places another gentle kiss on my lips. "Okay, fine. To be continued?"

"Possibly. If you're lucky."

I pick up my golf club and walk toward the exit. We have four more holes left on the course after our unexpected moment in the tunnel, and all of a sudden the place is packed with people. The family ahead of us are the slowest golfers ever, and the mother continues to shoot dirty looks at us while we wait for them to take their shots. Letting them pass us has slowed us down immensely, but damn, it was worth it.

Cal and I continue to exchange glances, and it's taking every ounce of strength I have to keep my hands to myself. In my defense, this night has been years in the making.

When we finally reach the last hole, I hit a hole-in-one again. I cheer loudly, "I won, I won."

"I guess it's your lucky night," Cal says, pretending to frown.

"I think so."

We barely get into the car before Cal's lips are on mine

again. He stops abruptly and leans his head against the head rest.

"I'm sorry, I just need to get something off my chest," he exclaims. "I know I said that tonight we'd have dinner as friends, but I haven't been able to stop thinking about you since that first night I saw you at the Hillards' housewarming party."

Okay, I wasn't expecting a full confession.

"And I don't want you to think I'm a bad person because I was still with Sara," he continues. "I told you we'd been having problems for a while. And honestly, I should've ended things long before I saw you again."

"But you didn't," I say softly. "I actually saw her at Diane's the other night. She made it clear that I should stay away from you and that you'd end up back together."

He shakes his head. "She cheated on me, not only with AJ but with another doctor too."

Wow. Poor innocent Sara really gets around. She definitely has everyone fooled.

"It's been over for at least a year," he continues. "I thought if I just threw myself into work then I wouldn't have to face it. I let it go on too long because I was afraid to start over again. And then you walked back into my life, and everything changed."

He turns back to face me. "Granted it was a long time ago, but I wish I could change the way I ended things with you."

I nod. "You broke my heart."

"I know. I was a dumb eighteen-year-old kid," he admits. "I let my ego get in the way when Theo told me he saw you with that Brent guy. I still hate him, by the way."

I grin. "So do I."

I reach up and run my fingers through his blond hair. "Who knows? Maybe things happened the way they were supposed to. You went to college then medical school, and we had experiences we were meant to have."

He brushes my cheek with his finger.

"So now what?"

I give a shrug. "I have no idea. Maybe we continue our friendship?"

He shakes his head. "I think it's too late for that—I'm throwing that whole friendship thing out the window."

I try to swallow the lump that keeps building in my throat.

"What does that mean?"

Without another word, he kisses me again. I think it's clear that Cal and I are quickly moving out of the friend zone. The question is—where do we go from here?

Chapter Twenty-Three

I'm not sure what I was expecting Cal's apartment to look like, but I'm actually quite impressed. It's really spacious for a one bedroom. Of course, he has the quintessential bachelor pad leather couches and large TV hanging on the wall, but otherwise it's decorated rather nicely. The walls are covered in artwork, and the kitchen has all the appropriate appliances, including a state-of-the-art blender and an air fryer.

"I know it's not fancy," he says, opening a bottle of wine.

"Believe it or not, it's nicer than I expected."

He pretends to wipe sweat from his forehead. "I was concerned the realtor in you was going to get all judgmental."

I laugh. "That's actually a valid concern because I tend to be. But in my defense, it's my job. I can't tell you how many times I've had to explain to clients that they have to declutter their homes just so we can stage photos. Their argument is usually that people are buying the house and not the stuff inside it—well, how the hell are they going to get a good look at the house, if you have piles of toys and junk everywhere?"

His eyes grow wide. "Damn, you're feisty when it comes to this subject."

I let out a puff of air. "It's one of my biggest pet peeves."

He hands me a glass of wine and asks if I want to head to the living room. When we sit down, he slides his arm along the back of the couch behind me. He puts on some background music, setting the mood for a perfect evening of talking and well—more talking.

"What made you decide to get into real estate?"

I tell him all about my passion, and how I remember the excitement of visiting homes with my mother when she worked in real estate.

"I couldn't see myself doing anything else," I tell him. "There's something magical about the moment a family buys their first home, or even better, their dream home. I think about how much I love the house I grew up in and want to be a part of that for someone else."

He smiles. "That's cool. I can't wait to buy a home of my own. It's just me—so I haven't been ready to take that step yet."

I sip my wine. "Sara was ready to take that step."

He puts his glass down on the coffee table. "Yes, well some of that was for show. She was very into how other people perceived us."

I place my glass down next to his. Sara is still the elephant that we need to talk about. I don't want to ruin the vibe we have going on between us, but it will come up at some point. I prefer to just get it over with.

"So, a few weeks ago I broke up with my boyfriend Jordan. He's a great person, but I knew I couldn't commit to him. There wasn't a specific reason other than, it just didn't feel right. I made a plan to take time to work on myself and continue to build my career."

He smiles. "Good for you."

I chew on my lip as I try to find the words I want to say. "I can't help but wonder if you need time to do the same."

He doesn't say anything for a few seconds, and the silence is deafening.

"You have a point," he agrees, his tone serious. My heart sinks at the thought of going another day away from this man. Ugh. Maybe I should learn to keep my mouth shut.

"If it'll make you comfortable, I'm willing to take a step back."

I open my mouth, but no words come out.

"But I want to make it clear that I'm doing it for you," he continues without hesitation. "I don't need time because I know what I want, and I don't have a single doubt about it."

"What do you want?" I ask, my voice shaking. I wonder if he can hear the pounding of my heart against my chest.

He nudges closer to me on the couch, keeping his eyes fixated on mine.

"I want more nights like this," he says, his voice thick with reassurance. "I want to get caught making out while playing mini golf. I want to have donuts at one clock in the morning. And I want to be with the dream girl I let go when I was eighteen."

How long can a person go without oxygen? I'm just wondering because Cal has taken my breath away. I guess it's a good thing he's a doctor.

Being a serial dater, I've heard some of the best, most creative pickup lines ever invented. Usually I have a snarky comeback, but in this moment I have nothing.

"What are you thinking about?" he asks.

I need to say or do something. At this point I have a few options—I could run, or I could completely give in and allow myself to be happy. Completely happy.

"I was just thinking that we should get donuts," I say nonchalantly.

He looks confused.

"I'm kidding—well, sort of," I say with a giggle.

I move to sit on his lap, straddling his legs.

"I think that I'm ready to throw all my plans out the window and be with the one man I've never been able to forget."

He takes my face in his hands and kisses me with more urgency than any of the previous kisses.

"You had me really worried for a minute."

"I'm sorry."

He puts his forehead to mine. "Now let's go get some donuts."

∼

I've had some wild dreams in my life, some of which have been very vivid. The worst are those dreams that are so perfect that you don't want to wake up. When I open my eyes, I shoot out of bed, panic immediately setting in as I try to remember if my evening with Cal really happened. My heart is racing as I wait for my phone to turn on. Peace comes over my body when I see the last text I received from him just a few hours ago. Holy crap, it really happened. I lean back against my quilted headboard and close my eyes.

It's not unusual for me to throw all caution to the wind and take a risk. I've been skydiving, swimming with sharks, and I jumped off a cliff in Maui. This might be my biggest risk yet, and I'm only slightly terrified.

It's almost ten o'clock, and I have a lot to get done today. I'm not looking forward to sorting through a bunch of old boxes, but maybe it will keep my mind off Cal and how freaking unbelievable last night was. I crawl out of bed and throw on a pair of leggings and a tank top.

Reagan and Gabby are in the kitchen when I finally make it out of my room.

Reagan is standing over a griddle, flipping pancakes.

"Are you cooking?"

She laughs. "I was in the mood for pancakes, but thankfully I only had to add water to the mix."

I breathe a sigh of relief. "Thank goodness. That seems easy enough."

Gabby raises her eyebrows at me, the corner of her mouth curling up. "Good morning, Lila."

I grab a coffee cup out of the cabinet. "Good morning, Gabby. Why do you have that smug look on your face?"

"No reason," she says innocently.

"Uh-huh."

"How was dinner with your *friend* Cal?"

I smile. "Okay, spill. What do you know?"

Guys talk even more than we do, so it wouldn't shock me if Theo already got the scoop this morning.

Reagan continues to flip pancakes.

"Let me think," she pauses, tapping her finger against her lips. "The only thing I heard was that it was one of the best nights of Cal's life."

Reagan raises one eyebrow. And in one instant we all scream in unison.

"Oh, my gosh, you guys—it was unreal," I gush, tears filling my eyes. "Everything about it."

"Holy crap, Lila's crying," Reagan exclaims, fanning her face.

"I'm not—oh hell, fine."

We all sit around the island and eat pancakes while I describe the evening, starting with the visit to Cal's parents' house.

"You guys got caught making out while playing mini golf?" Reagan shouts. "Oh, please don't give Jeremy any ideas."

My roommates swoon over Cal's admission, and I'm thrilled to relive every magical detail.

"Theo called Cal this morning to give him some news, so that's when he told him."

"News?" I ask.

She nods. "We set a wedding date."

That reminds me that Cal asked me to be his date to the wedding. Of course that was earlier in the evening before we really poured out our feelings.

"Oh yeah, Cal and I are attending the wedding together."

"I already called that a while ago," Gabby says knowingly.

Normally I'd be hesitant about so many people being invested in my relationship, but this is different. Gabby and Reagan are my family, the sisters I never had. And I guess that would officially make Theo my brother—yeah that's going to take some time to get used to.

"I have more news, and I hear I owe it all to you," Gabby says. "I met with Elizabeth yesterday."

'So, you're going to do it?'

She nods her head rapidly. "Elizabeth said it was your idea."

I shrug. "There's no one who could do a better job running Fun in the Sun in her absence."

Gabby throws her arms around me. "You're the best friend I've ever had."

Tears fill my eyes again as I pat her on the back. I don't know if anyone has ever said those words to me. I've always had a lot of friends, but I never had special bonds like I've formed with these two.

"Ugh. Enough crying for now. We have work to do."

I'm sure there are plenty of tears ahead in the coming weeks as we prepare to move. At least I know I have the best people by my side, and now I have Cal too. Is it possible for dreams to come true—maybe it is?

Chapter Twenty-Four

"Maybe we should just go with the second one," Reagan suggests. "It had the most space, and the view was to die for."

I never thought I could get tired of looking at homes, but after the third condo Reagan and I see, I'm over it for the day.

"I agree," I say. "Although any of them would be fine."

We sit down at a table in By the Bay Café to take a break from house hunting.

"And extra bonus, that condo is close to this place and the Pilates studio," she adds excitedly. I appreciate that she's trying to make a new place sound inviting.

"True."

She folds her hands and places them on the table. "I'm sorry, Lila. I know this isn't easy for you."

I sigh. "It's not, but like my mother so kindly reminded me—it's just a house, so I need to get over it."

The server stops by the table to take our drink order as I reach into my bag to retrieve my phone. I feel my face get hot when I see a text from Cal waiting for me.

Can't wait to see you later.

He's been working, so I haven't seen him since our dinner and mini golf adventure. I'm almost to the point of counting down the minutes, which goes against everything I would normally do after one evening with someone. It's safe to say that I've officially lost all control of my emotions.

"I'm assuming by the wattage of your smile that you got a message from Cal," Reagan sings. "Your face practically lit up the room."

Ugh. I didn't want to get all swoony, but I guess it's too late for that.

"It's really obvious and annoying, isn't it?"

Reagan shakes her head. "Not at all. You've seen how I am around Jeremy. When something or *someone* makes you happy, there's no reason to hide it."

"I know," I say. "I just never thought I would behave like this."

Reagan gasps.

"Calm down, it's not that big of a deal," I tell her.

"No, it's not that. But you better brace yourself," she whispers.

What? And why is she whispering?

"Reagan, yoo-hoo."

A shiver shoots down my spine. It's Bethany—and her voice is just as irritating as she is.

When I look up, I see her approaching our table with Jordan right behind her.

Oh boy, this is going to be fun. I almost forgot that Jordan and Bethany were spending time together, and I guess he hasn't grown tired of her antics yet. Despite my urge to drag him away from her, Jordan's personal life is none of my business. I can either make this weird or wish him well.

"Hey, guys," Reagan says politely. She's such a good person, we should all strive to be more like Reagan.

"Hi, Jordan. Bethany." My greeting doesn't come out as kind as Reagan's, but I should at least get an *A* for effort.

Jordan says hello, but I can tell he feels a bit uncomfortable. It's no secret that I'm not a Bethany fan.

"I was just thinking about you two," Bethany exclaims dramatically. "I really need to get back to that Pilates class."

Reagan looks at me and forces a smile. "Definitely."

"Well, we don't want to interrupt your lunch meeting,"

Jordan says, taking Bethany by the elbow. "It was nice to see you."

I groan under my breath. I can't believe I'm about to do this, but here we go. "No, you're fine," I say, fighting the urge to poke myself in the eye with my fork. "In fact, why don't you guys join us?"

Reagan chokes on her water. She probably thinks I've completely lost my mind—and maybe I have.

"Really?" Bethany asks. All three of them are staring at me with looks of utter shock on their faces, and I can't blame them.

"Yeah, we're not having a meeting. We just finished looking at some condos."

I don't mention Bethany's poor choice to spill the beans to Reagan about the move. It all turned out okay anyway, and there's no reason to keep dredging it up.

The server stops by to take our orders, and surprisingly Bethany is somewhat pleasant. She asks lots of questions about the places we looked at, and she even seems genuinely interested. I just hope Reagan proceeds with caution because she's been down this road with Bethany before.

Bethany and Reagan start discussing an old friend from Chicago, giving Jordan and me a chance to chat.

"How's life treating you?" I ask.

He smiles. "Really good, actually."

I nod my head in Bethany's direction. "Are you sure?"

He chuckles. "I know you two don't have the best history."

"Yeah, you could say that."

"Believe it or not, she's really trying to make amends with Reagan," he says softly.

"That's what I've heard," I say, taking a sip of my water.

"She knows she's caused a lot of turmoil, and she's realized that she doesn't want to lose the one person who's stood by her most of her life."

I glance over at Bethany who's showing Reagan something on her phone. This brings about the question—can people really change? Maybe she has seen the error of her ways, or maybe it's all a big act to make Jordan think she's a better person. Either way, he obviously sees another side of her, and so did Paul. She definitely has some influence over the men, and she knows it. I just don't understand why she keeps latching on to my friends. Miami is full of eligible men who would gladly put up with a woman like Bethany.

"I hope you're right," I say doubtfully. "Reagan is one of the best people I know, and I don't want to see her hurt by Bethany again."

He nods. "I think she's going to surprise you."

I let out a sigh. For Jordan's sake, I hope he's right. Unfortunately, it's going to take more than one lunch to make me join Team Bethany.

The remainder of our lunch is mostly uneventful, and after they leave, Reagan looks at me in astonishment. "Who are you, and what have you done with my friend Lila?"

My mouth twists. "I have no idea. I'm going with temporary insanity."

"It's something," she says. "First Theo and now Bethany. Cal Sims must really be having an effect on you."

I scowl. "Let's change the subject, please. I have a reputation to uphold."

"Whatever you say."

When I get home, I fall down on my bed and kick off my sandals. Between searching for a new place to live and being cordial with Bethany and Jordan, I'm mentally exhausted. A phone call from my mother is the last thing I want, so I take a few deep breaths before answering my phone.

"Hey, Mom."

"Hi, honey. How are sales?"

I roll my eyes and fight the urge to make a snarky comment. "All good. What's up?"

I stretch out on my bed while barely listening to her complain about a hotel they stayed at.

"We're looking forward to our family vacation," she says. "Once the house is sold, it'll be a huge relief."

It's so confusing to me that she has no sentimental attachment to our home at all.

"Aren't you even a little emotional about this?" I snap. "What about all the memories we have here?"

"Lila, I carry the memories with me every day," she replies. "Of course I'm a little sad. But I don't need a house to remind me of all the wonderful times we had."

I understand what she's saying, but I can't help but think about Cals parents' home and the walls covered with pictures of their family past and present. He's so lucky to have that constant in his life. The first thing he did when he finally ended his relationship with Sara was go home. Pretty soon, I'm not going to have that kind of stability. My parents are basically living in hotels right now while they have their own adventure.

"It's going to be okay, you'll see," my mother insists.

I remain quiet while she talks to me about painters and donation pickups.

After our conversation ends, I start to get ready to see Cal. The thought of this brings a smile back to my face.

∼

It's not often that I get weak in the knees, but Cal definitely has this kind of power over me. When I enter the living room, my pulse begins to race at the sight of him. He's wearing a tailored, blue sport coat and slacks with a crisp white shirt. His collar is open, revealing just a bit of his chest. This man should always wear blue because it really makes his eyes pop. I have no idea what he has planned for tonight, but he told me to dress up. I'm assuming that means we're not playing mini golf, although I'm sure we'll go back there sometime—if we're welcome.

Reagan is visibly trying to remain calm, but I know she's squealing inside.

I'm wearing a blush-colored, one-shoulder dress. It still had the tags on it, so I must have been saving it for a special occasion. I'd say my second second-date with Cal counts as special.

"Wow," he breathes.

"Dr. Sims, you clean up very nicely," I say coyly.

"I need to get ready too," Reagan says, making a quick exit. "Have fun tonight."

Cal doesn't move from his spot, but he turns to make sure Reagan is safely out of the room before he glides toward me.

"You just took my breath away," he whispers, before kissing me on the cheek and then moving to my lips.

When we finally let our embrace go, I run my hands over the outside of his coat. "I really like this suit."

"Thank you. I think the blue really brings out the color of my eyes," he says with a grin.

He must have been reading my mind.

"Absolutely."

He takes my hands in his. "Reagan told me you had an interesting day."

I laugh. "Yes. I'm definitely in need of some fun tonight."

"Well, I'm your guy," he says, touching his forehead to mine. "Tonight is just about us. Not to worry about anything or anyone else around us."

This is exactly what I needed to hear. Nothing else matters in this moment.

As we drive down to South Beach, Cal tells me about the last few days at the hospital. I have to admit that it gives me an adrenaline rush just listening to his experiences. Hearing how he held several lives in his hands makes me so grateful for those people who work tirelessly around the clock to serve their communities.

I reach over and touch his arm. "I'm in awe of how you can hold it together. How do you not completely lose it, especially seeing people in so much pain?"

He sighs. "I have my moments, but that's when I remind myself that I chose this field so I could help people. It keeps me level-headed and focused ... And over the last few days, I had tonight to look forward to."

He pulls my hand to his lips and kisses it, which sends a surge through my body.

A few seconds later we pull in front of a new steakhouse on Collins Avenue. A valet comes to my door and opens it.

"I'm sure you've been here before," Cal says, holding out his elbow to mine. "I know you're quite the social butterfly."

I roll my eyes. "As a matter of fact, I haven't, but I've heard fabulous things."

He punches the air with his hand. "Whew. I was panicking when I was trying to pick a place. I wanted it to be special, so I just spun the roulette wheel and hoped for the best."

I squeeze his arm. "That's very sweet of you, but anywhere would've been fine. I would've been perfectly content to go mini golfing again."

A mischievous grin spreads across his face. "Oh, we're going back there. I think we need another rematch."

As soon as we step into the lobby, a myriad of delicious smells fills my nostrils. The restaurant is warm and inviting with dim lighting and a hint of soothing R&B music playing in the background.

Cal checks in at the host stand, and I look around at the walls filled with mirrors and wine bottles.

"I'm impressed," I whisper, leaning into him. "If this goes well, you might end the night two for two."

He laughs and gives my hand a gentle squeeze. "That's the plan. I'm hoping I can convince you to go out with me a third time."

"Dr. Sims, right his way," calls the host.

I raise an eyebrow at him. "You're so fancy."

Cal and I sail through another meal, never running out of things to talk about. The food is fantastic. The only problem is, I'm noticing a tiny stitch of fear creeping up in to my mind, trying to interrupt my extraordinary night. Cal is everything I could ever want in a man. He's kind, service oriented, hard-working, and so gorgeous. So why am I worrying? I use all my energy to push this out of my head and just enjoy every minute I can.

After dinner while we're waiting for the car, a couple approaches us.

"Cal, I thought that was you," the man says, reaching out to shake his hand. A pretty woman behind him says hello while eyeing me curiously.

"Maggie, Dale, this is Lila Barlow," Cal says, placing his hand on my lower back.

We all shake hands, but it's obvious by their expressions they're wondering who the hell I am. Which probably means they're wondering why I'm here instead of Sara.

"I love your shoes," the woman says, pointing to my nude platform heels.

"Thank you," I say. "So, how do you all know each other?"

The three of them exchange looks.

"I work with Sara," Maggie says awkwardly then points to Cal and Dale. "These two like to get together to watch baseball. Thank goodness, because I can't watch baseball on TV."

Ah, she's a friend of Sara's. That explains the strange look she gave me.

"I can't wait for baseball season to start," Dale says, winking at Maggie.

Just then the valet driver pulls up with their car.

"Anyway, good seeing you, man," Dale says. "Nice meeting you, Lila."

"You too."

"Bye," Maggie calls.

Cal's car appears right behind theirs.

"I'm sorry about that," Cal says once we're in the car.

"There's nothing to apologize for," I say, patting his shoulder. "You're going to have friends who are connected to both you and Sara."

"I know. I just didn't want anything to get in the way of having a great time tonight."

I smile. "I am having a great time. Dinner was delicious, my date is wearing a super sexy blue suit—there's nothing more I could ask for."

We pull up to a stop light, and Cal leans over and kisses me. "You're amazing."

As we drive through the city, I peer out the window while my mind races. Is this moving too fast? Honestly, I'm terrified by how quickly I'm falling for Cal—or is it re-falling for him? Is that the correct term? I always knew that Cal Sims was never completely out of my system, but I figured he'd eventually fade into the distance along with the rest of my past.

"Dessert time," he announces, dragging me out of my thoughts.

I start laughing as soon as I see the familiar hot pink building.

"Do you think we're too overdressed for Sonny's Scoops?" he asks.

I laugh. "Most definitely."

Sonny's is an old hole-in-the-wall ice cream shop that's been open since the beginning of time—maybe even before that. It was a popular hangout when we were in high school, and honestly I had no idea it was still standing.

We get a few funny looks as we approach the window. I guess most people aren't wearing suits and designer dresses when they stop here to get a treat.

Cal turns to me. "Let me guess, vanilla soft serve in a cone with rainbow sprinkles?"

My mouth drops open. I'm impressed. How does he remember this stuff? "You got it."

Cal places our order and leads me over to one of the empty tables.

I lean my head to the side. "Okay, first the movie and now the ice cream. How do you remember all these things?"

He points to his head. "I'm a smart guy."

"Well, that's obvious, but seriously?"

They call Cal's name, so he runs to grab the cones.

He hands me my cone, and I hurry to taste it. It's as yummy as I remember.

"Okay, here's the deal. My dad gave me some advice years ago, and it's stuck with me," he says, wiping the corner of his mouth with a napkin. "He said to remember little details and never take time for granted because that's one thing you can't get back."

I nod. "That's some solid advice."

"It's always worked for him, so maybe there's something to it."

The thing about time is so true. You can't get it back. Thankfully you can make the most of the time in the present. Cal and I weren't in each other's lives for a long time, but he's here now. I don't know what's going to happen tomorrow or even next week, and that's what concerns me the most.

Chapter Twenty-Five

When we return to my house, Cal takes off his suit coat and sits down on the couch.

"Come here, let's talk," he says, patting the area next to him.

I sit down and start unbuckling my shoes.

"You've been quiet since we left Sonny's," he says, concern in his voice. "What's going on?"

"Shocking, isn't it?" I tease. "You should probably enjoy the peace while you can."

He gives me a half-smile. "Nah. I like the outgoing, fiery Lila."

That's good to know. Although he probably doesn't want to hear what's on my mind right now.

Tonight was wonderful, and once again Cal made every effort to make it that way, just like he did on our first date.

Maybe that's what's bothering me. Is this all too perfect? What happens if and when the novelty wears off? There's going to come a day when I'm in one of my moods and he realizes that I'm not the easiest person to deal with. Maybe he should talk to Gabby and Reagan and get a head's up?

I let out a puff of air. "Tonight was perfect, again."

He twists his mouth to the side. "That's good, right? Why am I sensing a *but*?"

I open my mouth, but no words come out. Instead something happens that I'm not expecting. My eyes fill with tears, and I quickly jump to my feet, so Cal doesn't see them.

"Lila?"

"I'm fine," I say, clearing my throat.

"No, you're not," he stands up and makes me turn around to face him.

"I hate this," I wail. "I don't cry."

Cal presses his lips together to keep from laughing.

"Don't laugh," I whine. "What I mean is, I *rarely* cry."

He leads me back to the couch and begs me to tell him what's bothering me.

"Honestly, I'm worried that this is moving too fast," I moan, looking away. I can't bear to look into his beautiful blue eyes. "You were with the same person for three years. Certain feelings don't just disappear overnight."

He groans. "Lila, I told you that Sara and I were over a long time ago."

I exhale and finally bring myself to look at him. "Yes, but what happens after we continue to spend time together and you realize that you didn't give yourself a break or time to mourn that relationship."

He rubs his forehead. "I don't want a break," he says, frustration in his voice. "I'm not sure what more I have to do to show you that I'm serious about you, and us."

I believe him, but my worries and insecurities are totally hijacking my gut. I've been known to back away before things get too serious.

"Well, what about when we run into more of your friends like we did tonight?" I ask. "I know that was uncomfortable for you."

He shrugs. "If they're my friends, they'll be happy for me no matter who I'm with."

My heart is racing as I continue to spit out the what if's.

He doesn't flinch or back down.

"I can be a real pain in the ass sometimes."

He snorts. "I already know that—it's not like we just met yesterday."

I scowl.

"Sometimes I'm impossible," he continues. "Especially after an exhausting shift with very little sleep."

Ugh. This is worse than I ever expected. I'm totally falling in love with Cal Sims and it's too late to stop it.

"This isn't going to be fun and exciting forever," I remind him. "You're going to get sick of me like you did before."

The words slip out before I realize it.

"Is that what this is about? Are you purposely pushing me away because you think I'm going to break up with you again?" he asks, concern in his voice.

"I don't know," I snap. "I'm scared, okay?"

My chest is rising and falling quickly as every bit of emotion I'm feeling finally comes to the surface.

"Why all of a sudden are you pulling out every stop to be with me?" I ask. "What about all those years? You could've reached out to me if you really wanted to—I certainly wasn't hard to find."

I can see the frustration rising in his face.

"I knew where you were," he says. "*You* were living your best life—all the parties, the yachts, the vacations. You became very successful, and you seemed happy. It didn't look like you were missing me from your life."

But I wasn't ever truly happy. Something was always missing. Maybe it was him. I can't be sure.

"I'm going to leave to give you time to think," he says, lowering his voice. "But just so you know. I'm not walking away from this until you tell me to."

He kisses me on the forehead and heads for the door.

I want to go after him, but I'm much too stubborn for that. It's probably a good thing. I should sort out my feelings because I don't want to mess this up. Not again.

∽

"Yes, it is the perfect floor plan for what you're looking for," I say eagerly. "I'll meet you there at three thirty. I know you're going to love this home."

I end the call and add the appointment to my calendar.

"We need to talk," Javier demands. "Some things are more important than work."

"What?"

"Um, hello. You're holding out on me, Lila."

I roll my eyes. "I'm not sure what you're referring to?"

He moves his chair closer to mine. "I've heard through a reputable source that you have a new man in your life."

I glance back at Gabby who's pretending to be busy. She's obviously the source he's referring to.

I haven't yet told my roommates about my last conversation

with Cal. Mainly because we've all been busy, and also because I don't want to hear their lectures.

The good news is that everything seems to be okay with him. He called to check up on me, and he said he wants to see me whenever I'm ready. After he left, I realized I probably overreacted. It wouldn't be the first time and probably won't be the last. At the same time I don't regret it because I had to say what was on my mind.

"I'll tell you all about it when—"

The office door opens, and we both look over. My eyes grow wide when I see Diane Hillard walk in. She gives me a wave, but her expression remains cold, which makes my heart sink into my stomach.

"Hi, Diane," I exclaim. "What a nice surprise."

"Hello, Lila, I was going to text you, but I figured since I was in the area I'd just stop by."

I'm sure she did. I have a feeling this isn't a friendly visit, judging by her unusually formal greeting. Diane isn't a good liar, unlike her niece, Sara.

"Well, you have great timing," I say. "Would you like to walk next door and grab some coffee?"

"Yes, that would be good."

Gabby looks up and gives me a worried look.

I grab my bag and walk outside into the warm sunshine. "How are you?" I ask.

She hesitates. "Well, um, to be honest I'm puzzled."

Here we go.

"Okay, is there something I can help you with?"

She sighs loudly. "Sara told me something very concerning ... I don't understand what's going on."

We walk into the cafe and sit down at a table near the window. She pulls a bottle of Mountain Dew out of her bag and takes a few loud gulps. I don't even bother to get a coffee or anything. I'm not expecting this to be a fun social visit.

"I need you to be honest with me."

I give her a nod. "I will always be honest with you."

"Sara says you and Calvin are seeing each other," she blurts out. "It doesn't make any sense to me, and I knew that you would be able to clear this up."

Even though I don't owe Diane or anyone else an explanation, I'm going to tell her the truth.

"Cal and I have gone out two times," I tell her. "I've known him since I was a teenager. We dated for six months when we were in high school, and he was my neighbor's best friend even before that."

She puts her fingers to her temples and stares down at the table. "How could you do this to Sara?" she asks, her tone full of disgust. "We welcomed you into our home, into our family. I encouraged you to be friends with her, but I had no idea you'd step in and steal her man. When she told me, I thought there had to be some mistake…"

I remain calm as she continues to berate me, even to the point of wishing they hadn't bought the house. Hmm, she's definitely reaching.

"I'm sorry you feel that way," I say calmly when she finally gives me a chance to speak.

"Oh, you bet I do."

"Well, I guess there's nothing else to say," I start to rise to my feet.

"That's it? You're not even going to have the decency to explain why you did such a terrible thing to Sara?" she says. "Calvin and Sara were happy. They were even willing to purchase your home."

Ugh. Not the house again.

"She wanted to buy my house, not Cal."

"Why does that matter?" she asks, raising her hands. "What kind of person breaks up a happy couple?"

"I'm not the reason their relationship ended," I snap. "Why don't you ask Sara about AJ Bennett?"

All the color drains from her face. "Sara and AJ are friends," she says, her voice shaking. "They have been for a long time."

"Ah, so you've met AJ," I say. "Why don't you ask Sara about the real reason they left my dinner party?"

Diane rises to her feet. "I don't appreciate you trashing my niece. It's a good thing our business relationship is complete because we're done here."

I nod my head. "I understand. Regardless, I'm glad I was able to help you find your home. I wish you the best."

She tightens her jaw and walks toward the door without saying good-bye.

Well, I think it's safe to say that the endless texts and calls from Diane Hillard are officially over. I didn't expect our partnership to end under these circumstances, but nothing surprises me anymore.

Chapter Twenty-Six

I've always been proud of the fact that I have very tough skin. I've learned to let things roll off my back, especially when people insult me. But for some reason, all the things that Diane Hillard said are bothering me. Even though I know that none of them are true, it makes me sad that she thinks so poorly of me. Not that I would ever expect her to take my side over Sara's.

I've worked with hundreds of families over the course of my career, and I've lost touch with many of them. I guess I'll just add the Hillards to that list and move on.

"How did it go?" Gabby asks when I return to the office. "I'm assuming she came to talk about Sara."

"Of course, and it went as bad as you can imagine," I say, sitting down in my chair and sliding myself closer to my desk. "She basically accused me of breaking them up and then stealing Cal away from her."

Gabby rolls her eyes. "If only Diane could've had the pleasure of meeting AJ."

"Oh, I think she has," I say. "Although she told me that Sara and AJ are only friends. I guess nothing is going to change her mind about her perfect angel Sara."

Gabby raises her eyebrows. "She'll figure it out sooner or later. The truth will always come out, no matter how hard you try to hide it."

Gabby's right. However, I'm not sure Diane would believe the truth if it hit her in the face.

As the day goes on, I'm trying my best to concentrate on my work, but I can't. I want to see Cal.

I grab my phone and send him a text.

Just wanted to say hi. I hope you're having a good day.

I stare at my laptop screen and think about what happened. Diane really pushed my buttons, but what she doesn't realize is how much I care about Cal. I would never do what Sara did to him. My phone buzzes, making my heart skip a beat.

I was just thinking about you.

A smile spreads across my face.

Diane Hillard just came to my office. It wasn't pretty.

While I wait for his response, my phone rings. I'm surprised when I see my father's number on the screen.

"Hello."

"Hi. How's my girl?"

"I'm okay, and sales are good."

I figure I'd just cut to the chase on that before he asks me. He goes on to tell me about a museum tour he and my mother just did and how their guide passed out and nearly fell down the stairs.

"That's quite a story," I say. "You and Mom have had some interesting experiences."

"Well, life is the greatest adventure you could ever take," he says adamantly. "And spending it with your soul mate makes it even better."

I smile to myself. My dad is hard core when it comes to business, but when it comes to my mother, he's a big teddy bear.

"Anyway, the reason I'm calling is to give you some news."

My body stiffens. I'm not sure I'm ready to hear any more news from them.

"What is it?" I ask cautiously.

"Drum roll …" He makes an annoying sound mimicking a drum.

"Dad?"

"We have a buyer for the house," he blurts out.

Um, what?

"That's impossible. I haven't listed it yet."

Am I hallucinating?

"I know. One of our contacts wants to buy it, and they've made us a very generous offer."

Is he serious?

"Dad, you don't know the market like I do," I insist. "We could probably get some great offers, possibly more than what we're asking."

Gabby looks over at me, her eyes growing wide. I guess I was being pretty loud. I can feel the tension rising in my body. Are my parents really in that much of a rush to sell it?

"I'll list it today. Let's just give it a little time."

"We've verbally accepted their offer, and believe me, it's good," he says. "Don't worry, I've done my research, and I think you'll be pleased."

"It's a better offer than you could've ever imagined," my mom shouts into the phone. "Just you wait."

Is this really happening? I'm not even talking about the house selling. I knew that was happening. I'm just beyond frustrated with my parents.

"Whatever," I snap. "Send me the buyer's info, and we'll get the paperwork started tonight or tomorrow."

There's no point in arguing with them, and I'm over it.

"Honey, I know this has been very difficult for you. We're not discounting your feelings," my dad says.

"I'm fine," I say. "I need to get back to work. I've got to get those sales in, and I need to sign a lease on a condo before I'm homeless."

"We love you," he says, avoiding my last comment. "And I promise everything with be okay."

I end the call and put my phone down on the desk.

"What happened?" Gabby asks.

I break the news to her that my parents have accepted an offer and there's nothing I can do about it. This day can't end soon enough.

~

As soon as I get home, I open the pantry and grab a box of Lucky Charms. Cereal is always there for you when you need it.

After seeing Diane and my conversation with my parents, I texted Cal and asked him to come over tonight. I'm so drained, and I think feeling his arms around me is exactly what I need. I don't know if we're going to figure things out tonight, but I don't care. I take my cereal outside to the patio and sit down on one of the chaise lounges. I listen to the soothing sound of the water running over the rocks in the pool and exhale deeply. It's actually happening—this house is almost gone. As sad as it is, I know everything is going to work out. Gabby, Reagan, and I will still be living together, Fun in the Sun isn't closing, and Cal is back in my life. And like my mom said, I will hold my memories in my heart no matter where I live. The one thing I can't control is Diane's opinion of me. The funny thing is that I thought I'd be relieved once we closed on her house and she was out of my life. I guess there's a part of me that enjoyed her friendship, and the constant praise was definitely a huge ego boost. Anyway, sometimes certain people aren't meant to stay in our lives. What's that saying about people coming into our lives for a reason or a season? I should look it up.

"Lila?" Reagan says.

"Oh, hey," I say.

She puts her hand on my shoulder. "Are you okay? You were staring off into space."

"Yes, I'm fine. Just thinking."

She sits down on the edge of the chair. "Gabby told me about your parents finding a buyer."

I shake my head. "Can you believe it? Their daughter is a hotshot real estate agent, and they decide to take the first offer that comes their way."

"Maybe it was just too good of a deal to pass up?"

I sigh. "It must be, because they won't even consider anything else."

I scoop up two marshmallows still floating in my bowl.

"We should probably move forward with renting that condo?"

"Yep. Let's do it." I pause. "Did Gabby tell you about Diane Hillard's wonderful visit?"

"No."

"It's been a really fun day," I say, my voice dripping with sarcasm.

Reagan's face turns red as I tell her about Diane and her accusations.

"I really want to call her and set her straight," she sneers. "She had no right to treat you like that."

"Thanks for wanting to defend me, but it won't make a difference. Diane will never go against Sara—she's the daughter she never had."

I bring my cereal bowl to the kitchen and tell her I need to get ready for Cal.

"I'm glad Cal's coming to be with you after the day you've had."

"Me too."

If only she knew about my mini meltdown after our last date. I could use a pep talk, but I really need to face this on my own. Cal says he's willing to take the risk and give us a try. The question is—am I?

~

When I open the door, I don't say a word and thankfully I don't cry. I'm not thrilled about this new crybaby version of myself. I'm wondering if all the years of not crying are finally catching up to me.

Cal immediately engulfs me in his arms and holds on to me for dear life. I must be crazy to even consider walking away from moments like these. I've been allowing fear to control me. It has to stop or it will rob me of the peace I feel when I'm with him.

"I'm so glad you wanted to see me," he says, kissing my hair.

I clasp my hands behind his lower back and don't let go. "I have so much to tell you, but first I want to apologize about the other night."

He puts his finger to my lips. "Nope. You had every right to express how you were feeling, and your concerns were valid."

I invite him inside, and we sit down on the couch. After my nutritious dinner consisting of a bowl of cereal and some grapes, I changed into a pair of black joggers and a cropped sweatshirt. Cal is still wearing his scrubs, and somehow he even makes those things look sexy.

I sit with my legs crossed and face him.

"Thank you for being so patient with me," I say. "I had the worst timing, especially after the night you planned for us."

"Yes, dinner and ice cream required a lot of planning," he teases.

"You know what I mean."

He laughs. "So talk to me about what happened with Diane."

I let out a long sigh and tell him about our unpleasant visit.

"I'm sorry you had to deal with that," he says. "Maybe I should call her."

"Why? So she can berate you too?" I ask. "You know as well as I do that she's not going to listen."

He nods. "Did she ever tell you the story about why Sara's so important to her?"

I shake my head. "The only thing she told me was that Sara was like a daughter to her. I can understand that, but she puts her on a pedestal that no one could ever compare to. No one is perfect."

"Diane lost a baby around the same time Christine had Sara," he explains. "That's why Sara means so much to her."

Oh, my goodness, that's heartbreaking.

"It's not a reason to excuse bad behavior, but that's why she feels this constant need to protect her."

"How tragic ... After Diane left today, I felt terrible. I complained a lot about the constant texts and calls from her, but there was a part of me that liked it. She called me more than my own mother does."

This reminds me about my conversation with my parents from earlier. "Speaking of my parents, they took it upon themselves to find a buyer for the house," I exclaim. "Can you believe it? They didn't even give me a chance to get photos or list it. I have no idea what those two are doing."

Cal gives me a sympathetic smile. "You've had quite a day. Did your parents give you a time frame?"

"Of course not," I wail. "They're taking this verbal offer, and when I asked my father if we could wait, he said no."

Cal pulls me into his lap, his strong arms wrapping around me once again. Silence lands on the room for a few seconds.

"Lila, do you trust me?"

I lean my head back and eye him curiously. "Where did that question come from?"

"Hear me out."

Something in my stomach stirs. Usually when someone says those words, it's followed by some grand confession.

"Do you trust me?" His blue eyes lock with mine.

"Yes," I say, my voice just above a whisper.

He takes his phone out of his pocket and scrolls.

What's he doing? Is he going to show me a picture? My stomach continues to twist as the anticipation grows.

He pushes a button and puts the phone to his ear.

Seriously? He picks this moment to make a phone call. What the hell is happening?

"Hey. It's me," he says, into the phone. "I'm with Lila."

He turns on the speaker.

"Hi, honey," a familiar voice says.

Wait—is that?

"Mom?"

"Yes, it's us."

My mind is swirling with tons of questions. Why did Cal just call my parents? How did he get their phone number? I'm so confused.

Cal has a gleam in his eyes, a slow grin spreading across his face. I'm still sitting in his lap, and he's running his fingers over my arm.

"What's going on?" I ask.

"Lila, we thought we should start working out the details for the sale," my mother says.

"Now? Mom what—"

All of a sudden I realize what's happening. I gasp loudly and stare at Cal.

"You?" I ask, a lump forming in my throat.

The corner of his mouth curls up. "It's a great house."

I cover my mouth with my hands.

Cal's buying my house. His was the offer my parents got.

"Cal contacted us a few days ago," my dad explains. "He got our information from Theo Jorgenson."

Theo was in on this too?

"I figured it'd be a great investment for the future. You and the girls can continue living here in the meantime … And then we can go from there."

"He made us an offer we couldn't refuse," my mother chimes in. "Honey, I know you're the best realtor in the state, but your mom still knows a few things too."

This is really happening. I can't even form a sentence. It's official—Lila Barlow is speechless.

"Are you still there?" my father calls.

"She's here," Cal says, rubbing my back.

"Yeah, I'm … processing."

"Why don't we call you back?" Cal says. "I want to talk to Lila."

"That's a good idea," my mom says. "We love you, honey."

"Love you, too," I mutter.

Chapter Twenty-Seven

*I*t's not often that I'm surprised. When I was growing up, I'd always guess my Christmas and birthday gifts before opening them. I'm usually very aware of what's going on around me. The events of the last few minutes might be the biggest surprise (or shock) of all time. After Cal ends the call with my parents, we both remain quiet.

"Are you sure about this?" I ask finally.

"I'm positive about all of it. The house and us." He exhales slowly. "I told you I was willing to do anything to show you how serious I am."

"But we're talking about purchasing a house," I exclaim. "And I thought you were against buying it."

I'm reminded of multiple conversations having to do with purchasing this house.

"I didn't want to buy it with Sara because I knew we didn't have a future"—he takes my face in his hands—"Listen, I can't guarantee that it's always going to be easy, but I know that I haven't been this happy in a very long time. Since you came back into my life, I feel like I'm alive again. And I have a really good feeling about what lies ahead."

My chest rises and falls as my heart starts to race.

"I don't have to leave."

He shakes his head. "No, you don't."

"And we're doing this—you and me."

He lets out a low laugh. "I really hope so."

I throw my arms around his neck and pull his mouth to mine, kissing him with every cell in my body.

After I pry myself away from him, I fire off every question that's spinning in my head.

"When did you decide to do this?"

"After our last date, I went to talk to my parents. I told them about your concerns, and my mom totally took your side."

I laugh. "I really like her."

He rolls his eyes playfully. "Anyway, we talked about everything you've been dealing with lately, and that's when I got the idea to reach out to your parents. I've been looking into investments for a while, so it wasn't an idea I pulled out of the blue."

"And Theo knows? What about the girls?"

"Yes, I talked to Theo about it. He had your parents' info, I guess for neighborhood emergencies. He thinks it's a great idea."

Wow. Theo continues to surprise me.

"The girls don't know. Theo didn't want to get Gabby's hopes up until we knew it was a possibility."

I still can't believe this. We don't have to move out, and it's all because of Cal. It's astounding how much life can change in an instant.

"I can't wait to tell them," I squeal.

"I have to know what my parents said when you called them," I beg. "I wish I could have heard that conversation."

He smiles. "Well, your mother was mostly concerned about our relationship. She even warned me not to hurt you again."

"Really?"

This is unexpected. I thought my mother would be more concerned about the business over my personal life.

"Oh, yeah. Then we finally got to the discussion about the house. I had no idea what to offer, so I threw out a few figures. The first one was too high, I guess. They were very receptive to the second, so we agreed on it verbally. Then I asked them not to tell you it was me—I wanted the timing to be right."

"You're good," I say. "You didn't let on to anything when I first brought it up."

"I wasn't planning to tell you tonight, but I couldn't let you stress about it any longer. I had some grand ideas about how I wanted to do it."

I run my fingers through his hair. "It was perfect."

I jump to my feet. "I think we should celebrate."

He raises an eyebrow. "I like the sound of that. Keep talking."

"We could go do something fun."

He stands up and takes my hand.

"How about miniature golf?"

I lean in to kiss him. "I love that idea."

∽

When I open my eyes, it only takes a few seconds to remember everything that happened yesterday. I sit up and stretch my arms above my head. I feel so refreshed today, like a weight has a finally lifted. Honestly, I have no idea how long I carried that weight around. Maybe years? I went about every day focused and driven, all the while feeling unsettled. When it came to relationships, I bailed out before I had to commit for fear of getting my heart broken.

There's no telling what the future holds for Cal and me, but I have no doubt that he's worth the risk. If he's willing to put up with me and go as far as buying my parents' house, he must be a keeper.

I hop out of bed and take a quick shower.

I left my roommates a note last night that we needed to talk this morning. I'm anxious to give them the exciting news that we don't have to move out. Cal and I called my parents back last night and discussed the details. I'm going to start the paperwork today, and then it will be official.

Cal had fun making lots of jokes about raising our rent and being a super strict landlord.

I twist my hair on top of my head and throw on a pair of skinny jeans and a fitted blouse.

Gabby and Reagan are sitting in the kitchen, discussing bridesmaid's dresses.

"Good morning."

"Lila will be the tie breaker," Gabby exclaims. "Lila, look at these two dresses. Which color do you like better?"

She turns her laptop toward me. The dresses are almost identical.

"They are the exact same color," I say flatly.

"See?" Reagan exclaims. "I told you."

Gabby frowns and looks more closely at the screen. "The one on the left looks lighter to me."

I pour myself a cup of coffee.

"What's up with you?" Reagan asks. "Did you and Cal have a good night?"

It takes all my effort to tone down my smile. "We did." I pause and let out a sigh. This is kind of fun—I should make it as dramatic as possible. "I have to talk to you guys about something. It's pretty important."

A look of panic spreads across both their faces.

"Is everything okay?" Gabby asks.

"Well, you know my parents found a buyer."

They both nod.

"When do we have to be out?" Gabby asks.

"We need to sign the lease on the condo today," Reagan reminds me.

"Actually, I don't know about that condo."

Reagan looks confused. "But we agreed that was the best option. Do we have time to keep looking?"

"Well, interestingly enough, we don't have to move out."

They give each other a look.

"I don't understand?" Gabby says.

"Cal's buying the house."

The room is silent before a collective scream escapes from both of their mouths. Of course the questions start, and I tell them about Cal's little sneaky surprise.

"Theo was in on it?" Gabby coos. "I love that man so much."

"Yes. Theo came through once again," I tell her. "I probably need to get him something, like a gift card or a fruit basket."

She giggles. "The only thing he wants is your friendship."

"Ugh. Fine."

I'm totally kidding. Theo and I are way past the issues of the past, but it's still fun to tease Gabby about it.

"More importantly, what does this mean for you and Cal?" Reagan asks. She's such a romantic.

I feel my face get hot. "You never know what the future will bring, but I'm feeling pretty confident that Cal and I are end game."

"Um, hello, the man is buying your parents' house," Gabby reminds me. "He's hooked for sure."

The feeling is definitely mutual.

"I'm so happy we get to stay here," Reagan says. "Although you'll be leaving before we know it."

Gabby's face falls. "Thank goodness I'm only going to be right next door. And let's be honest, I'll be here all the time."

We all get quiet for a few seconds.

"I just want you both to know how much your friendship means to me," I blurt out. "And I'm not going to cry, at least not today."

Gabby laughs. "Save your tears for my wedding."

"Oh, don't worry about that. You're marrying Theo Jorgenson, remember."

Chapter Twenty-Eight

"I'd like to make a toast to the best staff in the world," Elizabeth says, holding up her Diet Coke.

The day has finally come, and sadly she's off to London tomorrow. It's been a week since the announcement that Cal was the mystery buyer of my parents' home, and I feel like I've ridden a whirlwind. I've had a few closings, and we've all been preparing for Elizabeth's departure. Gabby is moving forward with overseeing day-to-day operations at Fun in the Sun, but for the most part we can all manage ourselves.

I think Suzanna was a little offended that she wasn't asked to take over the role, but she didn't say it out loud. I don't think she wanted to make Elizabeth feel bad, but I could see the disappointment on her face. I did overhear her make a comment to Javier about Gabby and me goofing off all day every day. Is she high? I have the highest sales in this office—I don't goof off.

The quick sale of my parents' home was an unexpected bonus, and they insisted I still take some commission on it. I tried to argue with them, because how tacky is it to take commission when your parents' sell their house to your boyfriend? It's kind of weird, right?

"I feel like I'm leaving my children behind," Elizabeth continues, fanning her face with her hands.

"You could always pay for us to come visit you, Mom," Javier suggests. "A trip to London would be a great bonus idea."

She gives a thoughtful look.

"We're going to be just fine here, and you're only an ocean away," I tell her.

All the color drains from her face.

Hmm ... maybe that was a poor choice of words.

I hear my phone ringing from my desk, so I hurry to answer it. My stomach twists when I see that it was a missed call from Diane. I didn't expect to hear from her ever again.

Curiosity takes over, so I walk outside to call her back. Crap, maybe she didn't mean to call me at all. What if it was a pocket dial?

"Hello," she answers.

"Uh, hi, Diane. Did you intend to call me? I just noticed that I missed a call."

"I did," she says, her tone cautious.

"What can I do for you?"

She fumbles over her words. "I need—um, I owe you an apology. My behavior during our last conversation was atrocious."

Whoa. I wonder what's sparked this sudden change of heart. Is it possible that Sara came clean? I want to ask, but maybe it's better if I wait for her to explain.

"Thank you, Diane. I accept your apology."

"I'm still very sad about how things ended, but I suppose everything happens for a reason."

"I believe it does," I agree.

"My Sara is healing, thankfully. She's going to be just fine."

I guess that's my answer. I have no doubt that sweet little Sara will land on her feet. She will snag herself another man in no time, if she hasn't already.

"That's good."

"I really do love my house, Lila," she says, her voice cracking slightly.

Hearing her say this brings a smile to my face. And like she said, everything happens for a reason. Maybe the Hillards were meant to come into my life—who knows if Cal and I would've reconnected if they hadn't. And to think, I almost didn't go to their housewarming party.

"It's a beautiful home, and I hope you make years of happy memories there."

"Thank you. Good Luck, Lila."

I hold the phone in my hand for a few seconds before walking back inside. For all I know, that might be the last conversation I ever have with Diane Hillard. I'm glad we ended on a better note this time, and one thing's for sure—I'll never be able to look at a Mountain Dew without thinking of her.

∽

"So, I guess this means we're going to be neighbors for a very long time," Theo says, giving me a wink. "What a great day."

I roll my eyes.

"Lila, it's okay to admit that you're really happy about it."

He opens the pizza box and adds two slices of pepperoni to his plate.

"Oh, yes. I'm so happy. This is the greatest thing to ever happen to me," I say in the most monotone voice I can muster.

He pats me on the shoulder. "It's okay. I know how you

really feel deep down. Expressing your true feelings can be difficult."

Theo ordered dinner for us to celebrate Cal's new home purchase and Gabby's new position at Fun in the Sun. Of course we all gladly accepted because none of us wanted to cook. Reagan and Jeremy should be home soon, and Cal is joining us after his shift ends.

"I'm going to change," Gabby tells us. "Is it safe to leave you two? You're going to be nice to each other, right?"

I grit my teeth. "I'll try my best."

As soon as she leaves, I take the opportunity to thank Theo for putting Cal in contact with my parents. I may enjoy giving him a hard time, but I'm super grateful to him.

"You're welcome, but if I'm being honest, some of it was purely selfish. It'll be awesome to finally have a friend living next door."

I giggle. "I figured as much. Who would've known that deep down you're a good guy, Theo?"

He smiles. "Lila, I think this is the start of a real friendship."

I snort. "It took long enough."

He shrugs. "Sometimes the best things are worth the wait."

Cal instantly comes to my mind. "You're right about that."

"And just think, someday our kids are going to be neighbors too. Do you think they're going to get along?"

Kids? Whoa, is he trying to stress me out? This might be the quickest friendship in all of history.

"Um, I have no idea," I hesitate.

"I'm sure they will be," he insists. "Theo and Cal part two. Can you imagine all the trouble they'll get into?"

"What are you two talking about?" I look up to see Cal standing in the doorway of my kitchen.

Did he hear us talking about kids? I will totally throw Theo under the bus. He's the one who brought it up.

"Ah, this is good stuff," Theo says. "We were just talking about our kids being best friends someday."

"Theo was talking about it," I insist.

I wait for Cal's reaction. He doesn't run out of the house screaming, so I guess that's a good sign. Instead he joins us and wraps his arms around me, planting a firm kiss on my lips.

"Or maybe they won't get along," Cal suggests. "Like you two."

What's happening right now? These men are talking about our hypothetical children being friends or foes.

Theo hands Cal a plate, and he opens a pizza box. He doesn't seem to be phased one bit about this subject.

Gabby rejoins us in the kitchen, and Theo fills her in on the conversation. She looks as confused as I feel. Believe me, I definitely want children someday. This just wasn't the conversation I expected to have over pizza with my old-new boyfriend and my former nemesis.

"How was your day?" Cal asks, finally getting off the kid subject.

"It was, interesting... Diane called me to apologize."

"Really? Good."

"She didn't say she was wrong about Sara, but she said she was sorry for the way she acted. And she thanked me for helping her find the house. I'm just glad she doesn't completely despise me."

"She doesn't. I think she knows the truth deep down."

Reagan and Jeremy arrive home a few minutes later and, as expected, Jeremy brought a big box from Donut Giant.

"Your boyfriend is a monster," Gabby says to Reagan. "Doesn't he realize that I have to fit into a wedding dress?"

Reagan giggles. "You don't have to eat one."

Gabby frowns. "Oh, sure. Like I could fight that temptation. I don't think I have that much willpower."

I smile as I look around the kitchen. I feel like I should pinch myself to make sure I'm not dreaming. Somehow I ended up with the best friends anyone could ask for, and Cal Sims and I are finally together. I always believed that good things could happen if you worked hard enough. But at some point I gave up on finding my happily ever after.

"What are you thinking about?" Cal whispers, his breath tickling my neck.

I lean my head back against his chest. "I was just thinking that I never want to forget nights like these."

"Don't worry, I have a feeling you're going to have plenty more just like this."

"I can't wait."

～

After the guys leave, Gabby, Reagan, and I are sitting on the patio talking.

"We really need to get moving on those wedding plans," Reagan squeals. "It's going to be so much fun."

Gabby forces a smile, but there's a look of sheer terror in her eyes.

"What's wrong?" I ask.

"Just nerves," she says with a sigh. "The last time I planned a wedding it didn't turn out so well."

"That's because you weren't meant to get married," Reagan says knowingly. "If you had married Dustin, you never would've moved to Miami and we wouldn't have met."

She nods. "You're right. I guess it was good that he cheated on me with my best friend."

"Former best friend," I remind her. "Maybe we should call and thank her for being such a horrible person."

We all laugh.

"I don't know what I would've done if you guys hadn't moved in here," I say. "I have no doubt my parents would've had this house sold long ago."

"That just proves that everything happens the way it's supposed to," Reagan reminds us. "I found the two greatest friends, and we've all found love."

"This house is definitely magical," Gabby announces.

"Maybe we should get Jeremy to buy a house on our street," I suggest. "Then we could all live near each other forever."

"And our kids can play together," Gabby adds.

Seriously? *The kid thing again?*

Gabby holds up her glass. "Let's make a toast. Here's to love," she says.

"And memories," Reagan adds.

"And friendship," I shout.

Love, memories, and friendship—there's always something to be thankful for.

Epilogue

*I*s there such a thing as happily ever after? Watching Gabby walk down the aisle and seeing how much she and Theo love each other tells me there is.

Gabby has officially moved next door now that she's Mrs. Theo Jorgenson, but she hangs out with Reagan and me so much it feels like she never left. She's also thriving as our leader at Fun in the Sun, which I know is a huge relief to Elizabeth. Meanwhile, Javier is still trying to convince Elizabeth to fly us all over to London for our monthly meeting with her. I'm so glad that she kept the agency open because even though I could work for any other company, it's where I belong.

Jeremy was visibly emotional at Gabby and Theo's wedding, and he's mentioned taking the next step with Reagan. We're trying to convince him to buy a house on our street, or at least in our neighborhood, and he keeps asking if I know a good realtor. That joke was funny the first few times. I can't be annoyed with him though because he supplies us with donuts every week, and who would be mad about that?

Paul says that Jordan and Bethany are still together and getting more serious. I wish Jordan nothing but happiness, and if Bethany gives him that, I have no right to judge. I'm still skeptical of her, but Reagan keeps reminding me that people can change. She's working toward trusting Bethany again, and although they may not be close friends, I believe they will come to an understanding.

It's so true that people come in and out of our lives for a reason. I'm grateful to have met the Hillards. They may not understand it, but my connection to them helped to lead me back to Cal. This being said, I know in my heart we would have found our way back to one another at some point.

Cal told me that he wants to marry me and that he will officially ask me when I least expect it. I have no doubt that he's the man I'm supposed to spend my life with, and I think I've known that deep down all along. I will absolutely say yes when he asks, and my roommates keep teasing me that it might happen at the miniature golf course.

My parents are planning our family weekend in New York City, and they invited Cal to join us. Ever since Cal purchased their house, they've been more present in my life, and they don't ask about my sales as much as they used to. I don't expect them to be as doting as Cal's parents, and that's okay.

Cal says he won't officially move into our home until we're married, so for now we are enjoying every second of making up for the years we were apart.

The events of the last year are a great reminder that life has many ups and downs and having people who stand by you makes it worth it. With friendship and love, making memories is what makes life so magical.

The End

Dear Reader

I hope you enjoyed *Thanks for the Friendship*. Please take a few minutes to leave a review on Amazon.

Love my books? Join my Facebook reader group. Interested in a free book? Click here.

Visit my website for updates, and stay tuned for my next book coming soon.

AuthorMelissaBaldwin.com

It Could Happen Now Available!

Buy It Could Happen on Amazon or read with your KindleUnlimited membership!

I don't like change. That's fine, because I, Tori Hayes, am quite content with my single status and fulfilling sales career. I'll make an exception and step out of my comfort zone to be a part of my college bestie's wedding party. Anything for a friend, you know?

But this—this is not what I thought it would be. Suddenly, I'm thrown into drama that only a Southern belle bride and her friends can stir up. The secrets, the lies, the deception—it's more than I can take. Not to mention that groomsman Tyler, who seems to know exactly how to push my buttons.

I don't like my buttons pushed. Or maybe I do.

Dashing groomsmen aside, why do I keep finding myself in the middle of all this madness? I want to support Caroline and give her the perfect day, but things are getting messy and fast. Is there going to be a happy ending amid all this chaos?

It could happen…

Love and Ohana Drama Now Available

Buy the first book in the Twist of Fate Series on Amazon or read with your KindleUnlimited membership!

Sometimes the most challenging situations bring the most happiness...

I'm Cora Fletcher, a twenty-something book-loving public relations executive, living with my overly Zen best friend and my attention-loving cat. I'm newly single and focusing on my exciting career, so I feel like I'm in a good place. I've even been invited on an all-expenses-paid Hawaiian vacation! The only catch? It's a family reunion... and my family can be a lot to handle.

But I'm determined not to let that get in the way. However, the ohana drama starts even before we board the plane. As usual, there's my sister-in-law, who's bent on causing friction, the self-centered cousins, and my aunt who loves to party a bit too much. My mom has filled the itinerary with endless activities, and she's even invited my ex-boyfriend in a misguided attempt to get us back together.

I feel overwhelmed, but then I get a blast from my past that could change my life forever. This is one reunion I did not see coming...

Will I make it through a week of family togetherness? And will I be able to say aloha to someone I thought was out of my life forever?

Love and Ohana Drama is a romantic comedy that explores the challenges of family dynamics and reminds readers that there is always hope for a second chance.

Acknowledgments

To my wonderful readers! You're the best! I hope my stories continue to bring joy to your lives.

To my awesome editor Wendi Baker, I adore working with you.

To Sue Traynor, thank you for another dazzling cover! You always "get" my vision.

To my husband and my daughter. I couldn't do this without you. You are my world!

About the Author

USA Today bestselling author Melissa Baldwin always dreamed of sharing her stories with the world. She brought this vision to life, becoming an award-winning, bestselling author of over thirty romantic comedies and cozy mysteries. Melissa is also a wife, mother, new empty-nester, and travel advisor.

Her books feature charming, ambitious, and real women, whom she considers part of her tribe. Although she rarely takes a day off, when she's not writing, she enjoys quality time with her family, traveling, attempting yoga poses, and booking Disney vacations. Melissa still uses a paper planner, and her guilty pleasures include Beverly Hills 90210 reruns and General Hospital.

Made in the USA
Columbia, SC
12 November 2024